BELONGING TO

Men of the Border Lands 1

Marla Monroe

MENAGE EVERLASTING

Siren Publishing, Inc.
www.SirenPublishing.com

A SIREN PUBLISHING BOOK
IMPRINT: Ménage Everlasting

BELONGING TO THEM
Copyright © 2011 by Marla Monroe

ISBN-10: 1-61926-214-2
ISBN-13: 978-1-61926-214-0

First Printing: December 2011

Cover design by Les Byerley
All art and logo copyright © 2011 by Siren Publishing, Inc.

Printed in the U.S.A.

PUBLISHER
Siren Publishing, Inc.
www.SirenPublishing.com

BELONGING TO THEM

Men of the Border Lands 1

MARLA MONROE
Copyright © 2011

Chapter One

Brandon loaded the supplies he and Bolton had obtained during their trip to Barter Town. They planned to make a stop in Skyline, the deserted city closest to their home, deep in the deserted outlands of west New America. Bolton walked up with a frown on his face.

"What's wrong?"

"I couldn't find a part for the pump."

"We'll look in Skyline when we go through. Not very many people salvage there with the wolves having taken up residence."

"I hope we find it. The one we're using isn't going to work much longer."

"Ready to load up and leave?" Brandon asked.

"Let's go. I'm tired of being here."

Brandon knew why his brother hated Barter Town. The women. They were little more than slaves here. Ever since the year of catastrophes, women were a rarity and highly sought after. In one year, floods, tornadoes, earthquake, tsunamis, and droughts had devastated the earth, toppling governments all over the world. All of this was followed by diseases that had killed even more. The United States, now called New America, had been one of the hardest hit. Now, five years later, less than a third of the population survived.

They started to load up when a noise caught their attention. They looked at each other and walked back around to where they'd closed the doors to their U-Haul trailer. Brandon threw open the door. A whimper came from the back of the trailer. Bolton climbed inside and cursed. He dragged out a female of about twenty-two years old. She had matted, reddish-brown hair and wore torn clothes a mile too big for her.

"What in the hell are you doing in our trailer?" Bolton asked, still holding her arm.

"Please. Take me with you. They make me do things."

Brandon closed his eyes. He knew what things. Two men ran a brothel of a sort with women they'd caught or traded for. Neither of them used it, because of the way the women were treated.

"I can't send her back there, Brandon." Bolton said the obvious.

"Ah, hell. Climb back in and keep quiet until we get out of town."

"Oh, God, thank you." She started crying.

"Shh. Get back in before someone sees you," Bolton told her.

She scrambled back inside the trailer and Bolton closed the doors back, latching them. They looked at each other then walked back to the truck and climbed inside. Brandon pulled out of Barter Town, hoping they'd made the right decision.

An hour outside of town, when there was little chance anyone would see them, Brandon pulled over. They climbed out once again to open the trailer doors. The timid female climbed out, squinting in the afternoon sun. She was soaking wet with sweat. Brandon cursed that he had waited so long to let her out. It had to be ninety degrees inside the trailer.

"You all right?" he asked.

"Just hot."

Bolton walked back to the truck and returned with a cool bottle of water.

"Drink it. You're dehydrated," he told her.

She grabbed the bottle and turned it up in desperation.

"Whoa there. Slow down. You'll make yourself sick." Brandon grabbed the bottle from her hands.

"I'm sorry." She cowered, looking down at her feet.

Bolton cursed.

Brandon gave her the water back, figuring she would be okay drinking the rest of it, but she was careful this time, only sipping.

"Let's get back on the road." Brandon turned to get back in the truck.

The woman moved as if to climb back in the trailer, but Bolton closed the door and grabbed her hand, pulling her around toward the front of the truck.

"You're not riding back there. You're riding up front with us."

"Won't someone see me?"

"We're too far out for anyone to come by now." Bolton urged her up into the truck.

"We're going to Skyline next. We'll get you some clothes while we're there."

Wide eyes turned to Brandon. "Aren't there wild animals there?"

"They won't attack you as long as you're careful. We're careful." Bolton closed the door.

Brandon started the truck and pulled back on the road heading toward the deserted city.

All three of them were quiet on the three-hour drive. Brandon noticed that Bolton kept looking at their addition as if he couldn't believe she were there. Having a female was a huge responsibility. They would have to take good care of her and protect her from thieves. There were men who would steal her from them, given half a chance.

Brandon pulled into the outskirts of Skyline around four that afternoon. They had another four good hours until the sun started to set. They had to make it quick. First stop would be an implement store for the part they needed to fix the well.

"I'll look for it. Why don't you two drive over to a clothing store for her," Bolton said.

"I don't like leaving you here." Brandon stared at Bolton.

"I'll be fine. I have the pistol if there's trouble."

Brandon sighed. It made sense to split up and grab what they needed, but he didn't like it. Nodding, he let Bolton out as close to the front door as he could get.

"We'll be back in forty-five minutes."

He pulled off as soon as Bolton squeezed through the doors. He looked over at his passenger and noticed she had moved closer to the door. She was afraid of them, but had been more afraid of her keepers.

He stopped at a Walmart not too far from the implement store. He drove up to the back bay doors that were pulled shut. He knew they were unlocked since he and Bolton had left them that way the last time they had been there.

"Okay, follow me inside. Don't run. If there are any wolves around, they'll chase you if you run, but leave you alone if you don't. Got it?"

The female nodded a little too rapidly for his taste. She was almost in shock. He hoped she would follow his directions. He was worried she hadn't really heard a thing he'd said. He got out first and pulled open the door. She climbed out of the truck and walked slowly toward him. Good girl, he thought.

Once inside, he closed the door behind her, and they were in total darkness. The skylights didn't start until you were in the main part of the store. He grabbed her hand and carefully negotiated the path they'd made before when they had been there, to the double doors that led into main part of the building. Once through them, the skylights offered enough light for them to easily negotiate the aisles.

"Let's find you some clothes. You'll need mostly jeans. Do you know what size you are?"

"I used to be a twelve, but things are big on me now." She didn't look at him.

"Better get the twelves, and try on some of the smaller sizes to see what you need for now. Once you're back home with us, you'll put your weight back on," he assured her.

They made their way to the right section and Brandon loaded her up with different sizes to try in thejeans. Once she'd found what actually fit, he got all they had in the two sizes. Then hegrabbed enough tops for a week. Nexthe moved to the men's section and found work shirts he thought would fit her well enough. He took the clothes from her.

"I'm going to put these in the truck. You gather up whatever underwear and female stuff you need. Grab one of the buggies sitting around."

"You're going to leave me here?" Her voice shook.

"You'll be fine. There aren't any animals in the store. We've been here several times gathering supplies," he assured her.

She nodded her head and looked around her. Brandon huffed out a breath and hurried to get rid of the clothes and get back to her before she had a panic attack. He found her pushing a buggy in the toothpaste section. Her buggy had a stack of underwear and socks, as well as probably most of the tampons they had in the store. She'd also gathered deodorant, toothbrushes, hairbrushes, and shampoo.

They searched for a plastic bin to carry everything in, and then headed back to the back of the store and the truck. Brandon loaded the bin into the back of the trailer,then climbed back in the cab of the truck to drive back and pick up Bolton.

When he pulled back into the parking lot, there were two wolves pacing back and forth in front of the doors. He honked his horn and pulled in between them. They backed up to the end of the drive.He glanced over at his passenger and found her shivering. She'd scooted over closer to him. Bolton came out of the glass doors carrying a box full of something and jumped in the truck, slamming the door behind him.

"We can pull over outside of town, and I'll transfer this to the back," he said.

"What all did you get?" Brandon asked.

"Found two of the parts we need for the well, plus some other things we might need as things wear out. Got some lubricant as well."

"Okay, anything else we need that you can think of?"

"Want to stop by one of the car dealerships and grab some batteries, or wait till next time?"

"Let's get home. We can do that next trip. We've still got a good five hours of driving," Brandon reminded him. "It will be close to eleven before we make it back."

Bolton nodded. Brandon pulled out of town with several wolves following behind them for about a mile.

"Why do the wolves stay there?" the female asked.

"There are plenty of places for them to make dens in the abandoned buildings."

"What's your name anyway?" Bolton asked her.

"Heather."

"I'm Bolton and this is my brother Brandon. How long were you in Barter Town?"

"I'm not sure, maybe a month?"

"We'll take care of you now," Brandon told her.

She only nodded and continued to cower between them. Brandon wondered how long it would be before she got comfortable around them. She was a tiny little thing compared to them. She might be five two and probably weighed less than a hundred twenty pounds. It was hard to tell much more about her other than she had medium-length reddish hair. The one clear thing about her was her blue eyes. They held shadows, but were the color of a clear spring sky.

"Where did you come from before Barter Town?" Brandon asked.

"I was in Texas, and got sold to some men heading to Barter Town. They traded me for something."

"Texas where you were from originally?" Bolton asked.

"No, I'm from Mississippi. Most everyone I knew died from the plague, so I and several others headed for Texas thinking it would be better there. We made it as far as the border when some men came along in a car and grabbed all of the women. They took us to some sort of compound where there were about twenty other women." She trailed off and looked down at her hands.

"Well, all that is behind you now," Brandon said. "We'll keep you safe. You belong to us now."

She nodded her head, but Brandon heard the sniff and figured there were tears to go with it. No doubt she was wondering if she'd ended up in a better situation or not. She wouldn't have any idea how they would treat her. Females were possessions now. Those lucky enough to have one should treat them like a precious gift and not like cattle, but most men were dogs and especially since the fall of the governments.

Brandon and Bolton were appalled at how women were treated now. They were humans just like men. They felt that they should be cared for and made to feel like the most important person in their lives because there were so few of them.

Brandon looked over at Bolton. His brother was having a hard time keeping his eyes off of her. They didn't really know anything about her other than what she'd told them, and he had no idea how much of that was true. Like it or not, she was theirs now to take care of. As much as he would like a female in their lives, Brandon knew they would have to protect her, and he wasn't sure they could handle the farm and watch out for her.

He hoped she would be able to help around the house. It would remove some of the burden from them if she would. Brandon wasn't sure what to expect from her.

All Bolton saw was a female who'd been used and abused. Brandon didn't have the heart to fill him in on the reality right now. He'd figure it all out on his own soon enough.

"Do you know anything about gardens or canning food?" Brandon asked.

"Yeah, I've always had a garden and put up vegetables. I can take care of a house and know how to raise chickens. I can't milk a cow, but I could learn."

Brandon was impressed. She might be of some help after all.

"We've got a garden, a few cows for meat and milk, and chickens. Got a few horses as well," Bolton told her.

"I'm a hard worker. I'll help however I can if you'll let me stay with you." Heather finally looked up at him.

Brandon sighed and nodded. "Like I said, you belong to us now. We won't send you back."

She seemed to relax at this, though she still didn't smile. Brandon wondered what it would take to make her smile. First thing though, she needed a bath and some clean clothes. She could bathe and dress while he and Bolton unloaded the trailer. It would be late, but he didn't dare leave it loaded. Thieves were everywhere now. They couldn't trust that they were too far north and out of the way for someone to bother them.

"Heather, when we get to the house, you can go ahead and take a bath and clean up. We have to unload the trailer. I'll bring your things in."

"You'll feel better after cleaning up," Bolton added.

Heather looked up at Bolton from under her dirty, matted hair and nodded.

"Can I have something to eat first? Just a piece of something? I haven't had anything all day."

Bolton cursed and looked out the side window before turning back to her.

"I'll get you something when we get home."

"Home? Will it be my home now, too? Or will you keep me locked up?" she asked, fiddling with her dirty dress.

Chapter Two

They pulled onto a gravel road several hours later. Heather was starved and tired. She had been hiding from the man running the brothel all day, and the stress of trying to stay hidden had drained her energy. Right now, she would settle for molded bread and a blanket on the ground. Not that what she had before had been much better. Now she had escaped the brothel to belong to two men she knew nothing about.

After another twenty minutes of driving the dark gravel road, they pulled into a clearing. The headlights from the truck illuminated a structure she couldn't quite make out. It looked vaguely like a house, but she wasn't sure.

Brandon stopped the truck and cut the engine. Bolton jumped out of the cab of the truck and held out his hand toward her.

"Come on. I'll get you something to eat and show you the bathroom. The water will be warm, but not hot, since we haven't been here to run the electricity."

"You have electricity out here?" Heather was surprised. Very few places had it anymore.

"We use solar energy with batteries to run the house." Bolton helped her down from the truck, then urged her toward the shadowy structure ahead of them.

"I'll be right in with her things," Brandon called out to them.

Heather turned to look over her shoulder at him, but the darkness swallowed him up. She nearly stumbled on a set of steps.

"Easy there. Watch out." Bolton caught her before she fell.

She followed his lead onto a porch and then inside the house. He picked up a lantern on the table by the front door and lit it. The flame threw shadows around the room, but she could see quite well. The inside of the house appeared to be an open floor plan. She could see all the way through to the kitchen from the front door. A set of stairs led up from the entrance hall, and a small hall curved around to the other side of the stairs.

"This way. Let's get you something to eat first." Bolton pulled her by the hand toward the kitchen in the back of the house.

He settled her in a chair at a table and disappeared from sight for a few seconds. He reappeared with a jar of peanut butter and a sleeve of crackers. He grabbed a knife and handed it to her.

"This should tide you over for now. I'll be back in a few minutes to show you the bathroom so you can get cleaned up."

"Thanks, Bolton."Heather attempted a smile despite still being a little afraid of him.

He just nodded and left her in the kitchen with only the light from the lamp in the other room. While she fixed peanut butter crackers and ate them, she heard the men unloading the truck and trailer. Several times, they came through with boxes or bags of stuff and sat them on the kitchen cabinets.

Once she had eaten all she felt she needed to, Heather cleaned up her mess and waited for Bolton to return for her. She didn't have long to wait. He appeared with the plastic bin containing her clothes and accessories.

"Follow me and I'll show you to the bathroom."

She followed him upstairs where he turned on a hall light as they stepped onto the landing. He then led her into a large bedroom through to a massive bathroom. He turned on a lamp in the bathroom on the counter and sat her things on the floor near the tub.

"Think you'll be okay by yourself for a while?" he asked.

"Yes, I'll be fine. I need to clean up, and that might take some time. I'm filthy."

"Take your time. I doubt we'll be finished before two or so anyway."

"Okay." She turned on the water in the tub and heard the bathroom door shut behind Bolton. She resisted the urge to lock it. They probably wouldn't like it if she did.

As soon as the water was deep enough, Heather stripped and climbed into the tub. It felt good to be able to sit in the water and just soak for a while. She leaned back in the tub and let the water cover her body. She knew she needed to bathe and get out, but she couldn't help wanting to enjoy the luxury of taking a real bath again for the first time in months.

She thought of the two men who had rescued her. Brandon stood well over six four, with shaggy brown hair that reached past his collar. His chocolate brown eyes didn't miss anything, and seemed to see right through her. She had no doubt that he would be the disciplinarian of the two men. His broad shoulders and wide chest thrilled the woman in her, but it also scared her. She had also noticed that both men had impressive cocks, if the faded white spot at their groins were anything to go by.

She couldn't help the way her body reacted to that bit of knowledge. Her pussy wept at the thought of all that male flesh filling her. She had little doubt that they would expect her to have sex with them. That was one of the main reasons men wanted women. Well, that and to clean up after them.

Her thoughts turned to Bolton, and how he seemed so different from Brandon despite their similar looks. He had black hair that appeared to be just as long as his brother's, and stood a little shorter than Brandon. They were both broad and muscular. Physically, they appeared alike. Their reactions and personalities were very different. Where Brandon was all business and serious, Bolton seemed to have more empathy, and appeared to be the more relaxed of the two.

Heather dunked her head and then worked shampoo into the matted ends. She scrubbed and threaded her fingers through her hair until she was satisfied she'd gotten all of the dirt and mats out. Then she dunked her head once again and let the water from the tub. Her hair reached just between her shoulder blades for the first time in over a month. She wrung it out then stepped out of the tub. Heatherused a towel to dry her body and then her hair.

Searching through the bin, she used the deodorant, toothbrush, toothpaste, and brush. By the time she had dressed in a gown and her hair was well on the way to being dry, Heather was worn out and ready to go to bed. She didn't have a clue where she would sleep. She cleaned up her mess before shoving the bin from the bathroom to the bedroom. Then she climbed up on the bed and curled up. She would rest for just a few minutes, then go downstairs and offer to help the men with their unpacking.

The next thing she knew, Brandon was picking her up. She shrieked and struggled to escape his arms.

"Whoa, Heather. I'm not going to hurt you. I'm just putting you under the covers so you can sleep."

"What time is it?"

"It's just after three in the morning. Bolton is showering and will be here in a minute."

"If you'll show me where you want me to sleep, I'll let you have your bed." Heather tried to pull from his arms.

"You're sleeping in here. This will be your room." Brandon pulled back the covers and slid her easily beneath them.

It was then that she realized he was nude. She quickly averted her eyes and shivered. She had been right. His cock was huge, and it jutted out as if looking for her. Surely they didn't plan on having sex with her right then. Was she in any better place than the brothel? Reluctantly, she acknowledged that she was. At least here she only had two men to please, and it would always be the same two, and not lots of different ones. How hard could it be to take care of them?

Resigned, she sighed and huddled beneath the covers as if it were cold in the room. She watched as Brandon climbed in on one side. He turned toward her and pulled her closer to him. Heather expected him to start undressing her, but he only wrapped an arm around her waist and tucked her head beneath his chin.

"Get some rest, Heather. Tomorrow will be a long day. We have a lot of unpacking to do, and the farm to take care of."

Confused, she tried to relax, but a noise from the other side of the room let her know that Bolton had walked out of the bathroom and headed for the bed. She nearly jumped when the other side of the bed dipped, and heated male flesh came in contact with her legs.

"Easy there. We're not going to hurt you. Calm down and relax. You need to rest," Brandon said again.

"I don't understand."

"Don't understand what?" Bolton asked in a weary voice.

"I thought, I thought you would want sex."

"Not tonight, that's for damn sure. I'm too tired." Bolton chuckled.

"That monster you call a cock is poking me in the stomach."

"Do you want to have sex?" Brandon asked from behind her.

"No! I mean…" She couldn't think what to say.

Did she want to have sex with these two men? Honestly, yes, but because she wanted to, and not because she had to. She doubted they would understand that.

"Just go to sleep, woman." Brandon yawned and pressed tighter against her.

She was surrounded by male bodies. Still, somehow she managed to fall asleep.

* * * *

Heather woke alone in the massive bed. She had no idea what time it was, or where the men were. By the amount of light outside the window, it had to be late morning. She hurried through her morning routine and dressed in a pair of new jeans and a T-shirt that actually fit her. She pulled on socks and the boots she'd been wearing the night before.

It didn't take her long to tidy up the bed and make her way downstairs to the kitchen. She rounded the corner and found the two men drinking their cups of coffee, talking. They fell silent as soon as they realized she was there.

"Morning, Heather," Bolton said. "Want some coffee?"

"Um, no thanks. I don't drink coffee." She hovered in the doorway, unsure what to do.

"Come on in and have a seat. We were just trying to decide what we needed to do first. It's already after nine." Brandon pulled out a chair between them.

"Would you like me to cook something for breakfast?"

"There's biscuits and gravy on the stove if you're hungry. We've already eaten. You can fix something for lunch later," Bolton said.

"Come on, have a seat." Brandon patted the chair bottom he had pulled out.

Heather crossed the room and sat down, fiddling with her T-shirt. She hadn't realized before just how big the two men appeared to be. They each dwarfed her.

"I figure you and Bolton can unpack the supplies here in the house, and I'll work outside today. You can call me when lunch is ready." Brandon turned up the cup and drained the last of his coffee. "Best get going. We've got a lot waiting on us."

"Come on, Heather. I'll fix you a plate. You've got to eat, or you'll never last the morning." Bolton stood up as Brandon walked out the back door.

"I'll fix my own plate. You get to work, and then I'll join you and you can tell me what to do." She jumped up and hurried to the stove. "Uh, Bolton? Why is the gravy red?"

He laughed from the other side of the kitchen. "It's tomato gravy. It's good. Warm it up and pour it over your biscuits."

She shrugged and followed his instructions. He was right, it was good. She cleaned her plate then cleaned up the kitchen. She found Bolton in a large pantry unpacking a box of dry goods.

"Why don't you let me do that? I can figure out where to put stuff. I need to know, because I'll probably be doing the cooking from now on."

Bolton nodded and climbed off the ladder. "Be careful. Don't fall and break your neck."

As soon as he left her alone in the pantry, Heather could breathe again. He took up so much room. She spent the better part of the next hour putting away groceries. When she was finished, she wondered where Bolton had gone. She didn't know what to do next. She dragged the empty boxes out of the pantry and stacked them by the back door. She was sure they would need to use them again.

"You finished?"

She nearly screamed when Bolton suddenly appeared behind her.

"God, don't do that."

"Do what?" He walked over to the sink and filled a glass with water.

"Sneak up on me."

"I thought you heard me walk into the room. I wasn't trying to be quiet." He drained the glass and filled it up again.

Heather watched the muscles of his throat work and realized she was staring at him. She quickly looked away.

"What do I need to do next?"

"Come on upstairs and I'll show you." He left the glass by the sink and led the way to the stairs.

Here it comes, the sex. They'll each corner me every chance they get and use me. Heather sighed and followed him upstairs, wondering if she should start undressing, or if he wanted to do it.

He turned to say something, then frowned. "Hey, you don't have to if you don't want to. We can move our own clothes later."

"What?" Totally confused, Heather jerked to a stop.

"Move our clothes. What did you think I wanted you to do?" Then it must have dawned on him because his brows knit together in anger.

"Fuck! You think I brought you up here to fuck you?"

"That's why you kept me, isn't it?"

"Hell, no. We *helped* you get away because you don't deserve to be treated like a slave. There was no way we were going to leave you to some bastard that would abuse you."

"I don't understand. I belong to you now. Your brother said so." She wrapped her arms around her middle, a little afraid of Bolton in the mood he was in now.

"Yes, but you belong to us because you have to belong to someone, or you're free for anyone to grab. You're our responsibility, but we'll take good care of you. We aren't going to attack you for sex."

"You don't want me?"

"Hell, females are so complicated," Bolton said under his breath.

"I mean, last night, you were hard."

"Yes, we want you, but not until you're comfortable around us. We aren't animals, Heather."

"Okay." She bit her lower lip and waited for him to tell her what to do.

When he groaned and turned away, she was confused again, but waited for him to say something. She didn't want to make things any worse.

"What I wanted you to do was put your things up in here, and move our things out of the other two bedrooms into here as well. We'll all stay in here from now on. It's safer to be together." He took her hand and pulled her out of the master bedroom, and showed her the other two rooms where their things were. "Can you do that?"

"Sure. I'll do that. Where will you be?"

"I'm going to unload the rest of the stuff off the back porch that goes in the cellar. I'll show that to you after lunch."

"What do I fix for lunch? What do you normally eat?"

"There's fresh-cut bread we picked up while we were in town. You can make peanut butter sandwiches for us. We've got to use up the peanut butter before it goes bad." He walked toward the door, then stopped and turned around.

"Heather, we want you. Don't think we don't, but nothing is going to happen until you're ready. We won't force you." Then he walked through the door and left her to sort out the bedrooms.

She sighed, and hoped he was telling her the truth. She liked what little she knew of them so far, and wanted to feel safe. So far they hadn't done anything to harm her, and had fed her and let her bathe. She should feel grateful and offer to take care of their sexual needs without them asking, but she was nervous. Her life could be so much worse, and had been. Even before the year of catastrophes, she'd felt beholden to her foster parents since they always told her they took her in out of the kindness of their hearts. She felt like she had to be the very best girl she could be to make them love her.

She spent the next two hours combining the two bedrooms into the one master bedroom. There was plenty of room for everyone's clothes, with plenty of room left in the closets. They each had three pair of boots and several pair of tennis shoes. She had only the one pair, and cursed that she hadn't thought to get some more shoes while at the store the day before. Maybe they would go back before long, and she could get more shoes.

She decided it had to be close to time for lunch since her stomach began to growl. She hurried downstairs to make sandwiches. She made two for each of the men and one for herself, then walked outside the back and called Bolton. Both men walked up from what looked like a barn out back.

"Um, lunch is ready. Do you have a clock anywhere so I will know what time it is?"

Brandon pointed to one hanging over the kitchen sink. "You mean like that one?"

They all three laughed, and the mood lightened. The men talked about the garden and how they would enlarge it next spring. This year it was all they could handle with everything else they had to tend to.

"I'll show you the garden when I show you the rest of the place," Bolton told her.

"Do you have canning supplies?" she asked.

"Do you know how to put up vegetables?" Brandon asked, the unmistakable sound of hope in his voice.

"Yes. I was raised by my grandmother. Remember, I told you last night, but I'm sure you were tired. We put up all sorts of things all year long. If you have canning supplies, I can put it up."

"Hot damn!" Brandon grabbed her and kissed her full on the lips.

She realized she liked it when he kissed her. But it was over with almost as fast as it began.

"We've got some, but we can get tons more," Bolton told her. "Everything you should need is in the cellar. I'll show you."

"Go ahead and show her the rest of the place. I'll take care of the animals while you do. You can finish up the chores later." Brandon smiled at her for the first time since she'd met him. He actually had a dimple in the corner of his cheek when he smiled.

"Come on, Heather. Let me show you the cellar first." He took her hand and pulled her toward another room behind the kitchen that housed a huge wash sink and clothesline.

He showed her the cellar door and opened it. He reached to the right and turned on a light. A set of stairs led downward. He started down the stairs. When she didn't follow him, he looked back at her with a questioning look.

"I'm not sure I can go down there. I don't like close places."

"You got in our trailer easy enough," he pointed out.

"Yeah, but I was more scared of where I'd been." She shoved her hands in her pockets.

"Come on. You'll be fine. I'm down here with you, and the light is on." He took another step down.

Heather drew in a deep breath then took a step down. She swallowed and took another, and another, until she stood at the bottom of the stairs beside Bolton.

"Good girl." He led her around and pointed out everything.

"You don't have much in the way of vegetables put away."

"We didn't know how to do it, and didn't have the time. What we have, we bartered for."

"Show me the garden." She shivered. Though it felt cool down there, she was ready to go back up.

"You first." He pointed to the stairs and followed her as she scrambled up the steps.

She heard him chuckle behind her. She turned around and stuck her tongue out at him. He full-out laughed at that. She found she liked the sound of his laugh.

She followed him outside and behind the house to a large, open area. Here they had planted a garden that was in full bloom and stretched a good hundred yards long by fifty yards wide. She recognized tomatoes, corn, peppers, green beans, and purple hull peas. It looked as if there were some things that needed picking now.

"I think I need to work in the garden some today. Is that okay with you?" She turned to Bolton.

"Sure, if you want to, but don't get too hot. Drink plenty of water. It's nearly two in the afternoon. I don't want you to get sick."

"I'll be fine." She smiled and hurried back to the kitchen, where she grabbed a knife and a bucket. This she could handle.

Bolton watched her for a few minutes, then shrugged and walked off to tend to whatever needed his attention.

She gathered tomatoes, peppers, and enough beans to cook that night. She decided the purple hulls needed another day before they would be ready. After washing the bounty, she searched the kitchen to learn where everything was located. She found flour, cornmeal, sugar, and an assortment of spices. She searched for meat and found the fridge actually worked, though it didn't freeze anything. It only kept things cold.

If the men were anything like her grandfather had been, they wouldn't come in until dark. She spent the rest of the afternoon learning the house and where everything was kept. By the time the men returned, she had supper on the table. They praised her over the meal and offered to help clean up. She shook her head and they moved into the living area, where she heard them talking about the farm.

While she cleaned up, she listened to them discuss the day's events and what their plans were for the next day. She would love to feel a part of that.

When she had finished in the kitchen, she hovered in the doorway, wondering what she needed to do next. Brandon looked up and gestured for her to join them.

"Come on over here. We'll go to bed soon, as we need to be up early in the morning."

Bolton smiled at her and ruffled her hair. "How was your first day in your new home?"

Heather smiled. Home. She hadn't thought she would ever have one again.

"Nice. It was nice."

Chapter Three

Brandon watched the smile bloom across Heather's face. She liked the idea of having a home. They would do everything they could to make sure she always felt that way. He hoped that they would become a family soon. He knew he wanted her with a vengeance. His cock had been hard nearly all day, making working a painful experience. He knew Bolton felt the same way. She was lovely to look at now that she was cleaned up.

Her beautiful red hair shone in the sunlight when she had been working in the garden. He'd stopped to watch her for a while. When she bent over, checking the peas, her rounded ass beckoned to him. He loved heart-shaped ass as much as Bolton loved big tits, and she had a nice set on her.

She was sitting close enough he could smell honeysuckle. It must be her soap she'd used, or maybe the shampoo. Whatever it was, it pleased him. They were all dirty and needed showers after working all day. It didn't take away from her attraction, though. He still wanted her.

"How about calling it a night," he suggested. "I'm ready for a shower."

"Water ought to be fairly warm, too," Bolton added.

"Won't be enough for all three of us though," Brandon pointed out.

"We can shower together, then." Bolton stood up and stretched. "It'll save on water, and make sure we all get some warm water to clean up in."

"Together?" Heather squeaked.

Brandon smiled to himself. She was still antsy around them. He hoped to settle that tonight. They wouldn't force her or even push her very far, but they would try and seduce her. He and Bolton had talked about it, and felt the anticipation for her was driving her crazy. They didn't want her all wound up over it. They would try seducing her. If she relaxed enough and was agreeable, then it would happen. But if she wasn't, they wouldn't force her.

"Yeah, just bathe, Heather."

"I—I suppose." She swallowed hard and stood up to follow them upstairs.

They stripped in the bedroom, with Heather waiting until they had disappeared in the bathroom to undress. Brandon smiled over at Bolton as he turned on the water to adjust the temperature. It was plenty warm for them.

"Come on, Heather, or you'll miss the warm water," he called out.

He and Bolton went ahead and got in the large, walk-in shower and began soaping up. Heather eased around the corner as if afraid to show herself.

"It's okay, Heather. We aren't going to attack you." Brandon tossed her a wet bath cloth, laughing when it struck her square in the chest.

"I'm not used to bathing with men," she confessed.

"Get used to it. It saves on water, especially in the winter. You'll appreciate it," Bolton added.

"Come here and let me soap up your back for you." Brandon held up the soap.

Heather hesitated but then walked in and turned her back to him. He knew how difficult it had been for her to join them naked in the shower. He grinned over at his brother and began spreading soap on her back. Then he added his cloth and washed her back for her. He scrubbed, knowing it would feel good. Then he moved lower and scrubbed her ass. She started to protest, but kept quiet.

"Okay, turn around and rinse off. You can soap my back while you rinse." Brandon turned around and flipped the cloth over his shoulder at her.

Heather laughed and popped him on the ass with it.

"Hey, that will cost you."

She just chuckled and began washing his back. She dug in and massaged his shoulders for him, as well as his lower back. She skipped his ass, though, and told him to rinse.

"My turn." Bolton presented his back to her and waited. She looked over at Brandon, then shrugged and treated his brother to the same thorough scrubbing and massage.

"Man that felt good. Thanks, Heather." Bolton soaped up his hands and before she realized what he was about to do, he'd begun spreading the soap over her breasts.

"I—I can do that," she whispered.

"I know, but it's more fun for me to do it."

Brandon soaped up his hands and wrapped his arms around her from behind. His cock stood at attention and snugged between her ass cheeks as he ran his soapy hands over her abdomen and thighs. She whimpered, but didn't protest.

Brandon knew the minute his brother had begun tugging and pinching her nipples. She leaned back into him, moaning. He took that as the sign he needed to move lower to her sweet pussy. He rinsed his hand around Bolton and began circling her pussy with his fingers. He delved between her pussy lips and brushed over her clit. She moaned and leaned further back against him. He braced his legs to hold her

"Let me rinse her off, Brandon." Bolton adjusted the showerhead to let the water rain down on her. Then he turned it off and took a nipple into his mouth.

Brandon ran two fingers into her slit and found her juices beginning to flow. She was with them. He nodded at his brother to let him know she was enjoying their attention. A few more minutes of pleasuring her, and they would quickly dry her off and continue the assault in the bedroom. He couldn't wait to taste her sweet pussy. He could imagine her cunt would be soaked by then.

She pressed her breasts closer to Bolton as he sucked and nipped at them. She ground her ass against Brandon's cock, causing him to grind his teeth at the pleasure.

"I think we need to move this to the bedroom, brother." Bolton stepped out of the shower, much to Heather's obvious displeasure.

She grunted and followed him without being told. He grabbed a towel and began patting her dry. Brandon grabbed another towel and quickly dried off. He picked her up to carry her to the bed while his brother dried off. She held on to him, but didn't protest. When he dropped her on the bed, she giggled and scooted up into the center.

Bolton joined them and immediately went after her tits again. He latched onto one, drawing an immediate "ah" from Heather. Brandon shouldered his way between her legs and blew across her cunt with a warm breath. She bent her legs and let them fall apart, giving him better access to her sweet pussy lips. He placed openmouthed kisses against her sex. She tilted her pelvis to get closer to him.

"You taste like honey. I could make a meal off of your sweet pussy." He stiffened his tongue and began to slowly fuck her with it. She whimpered and tried to fuck him back with her hot cunt.

He looked up and found his brother kissing along her neck and shoulders now while he pinched and pulled on her breasts. She turned her head as if in search of his mouth, and when he realized it, he took it. The sight of them kissing caused his dick to throb and his balls to tighten.

Using a finger, he carefully entered her wet pussy and found her hot and tight. He pumped it in and out for a few seconds, then added a second finger to stretch her. She would be so fucking tight on his cock. He curled his fingers in search of her hot spot, wanting to be sure she came before they fucked her. She jerked when he located it,and began a soft keening noise. He looked up and found that Bolton was back at her breasts again.

Brandon gently stroked her G-spot and sucked on her clit at the same time his brother pulled on her nipples. Heather exploded around him. She milked at his fingers with her tight cunt as if trying to hold him inside of her. He couldn't wait to feel her do that to his cock.

Before she had even calmed down, Brandon climbed up and lifted her hips to align his cock with her slit. He began pushing in even as Bolton massaged her breasts, whispering softly in her ear how good she was. Brandon slowly fucked in and out of her until he was balls deep, touching her womb. He held himself still as she adjusted to him. Her wide eyes told him he filled her. Her tight vaginal muscles swelled around him. He gritted his teeth as he waited for her to relax.

When she began moving against him, he knew she was ready. He pulled out and pushed in, in long, slow strokes until she was grunting and lifting her pelvis to urge him faster. He smiled and gave her what she asked for. He sped up and began thrusting over and over inside of her. He wasn't going to be able to hold on. It had been too long, and she was so fucking tight. He reached between her pussy lips and found her clit and tapped it. She reacted immediately, wrapping her legs around his waist and screaming her release.

Brandon held himself inside of her as he shot streams of cum deep inside her sweet cunt. They both collapsed against the bed. Bolton stroked her shoulders and arms until she'd caught her breath. Before Bolton could move, she'd rolled over and latched onto his cock with her mouth. He groaned and stroked her head.

Brandon felt his dick harden all over again watching her bob up and down on his brother's dick. She licked around the rim of the mushroom head before sucking it down again. The ecstasy on his brother's face proved that she was good at sucking cock. When he could take it no longer, he gently extracted his dick from her questing mouth and told her to get on her hands and knees.

Heather didn't hesitate. She rolled over and presented her ass to his brother. She looked over her shoulder with heavy-lidded eyes. Bolton positioned himself behind her and pulled her ass cheeks apart. Brandon licked his lips at the sight of her dark rosette. He wanted her ass, but figured it would be some time before she would be ready for that.

Bolton plunged inside of her wet pussy and began pounding into her with a look of bliss on his face. Brandon could well understand it. She was tight, and in that position, he would be able to go deeper into her hot cunt.

He watched as Heather began shoving back against Bolton as hard as he tunneled inside of her. At this rate, his brother wouldn't last much longer. He reached beneath Heather and fingered her clit to help her reach her climax at the same time as his brother. He knew what it felt like to have her vaginal muscles milk his cock.

In seconds, she was crying out. His brother lost his rhythm and came at the same time. He held himself there for long seconds before he collapsed over Heather. Brandon smiled and pulled him off of her before he suffocated her. He went to the bathroom and brought back a wet cloth to clean Heather of their seed so she would sleep comfortably. Then he crawled into bed on the other side of her and pulled her into his arms. She sighed and wrapped her arms around Bolton. They'd made progress tonight. She would soon relax and become the center of their family.

Brandon remained awake for a long time, just enjoying the feel of her in his arms and the knowledge that she was theirs. He would do everything in his power to assure she was happy. She made his brother smile, and satisfied him in ways he never thought he would be satisfied. As head of the family, it meant more responsibility, but he would gladly shoulder it to have his group content and safe.

* * * *

After several weeks of feeling each other out and become more used to each other and their little idiosyncrasies, Heather truly felt comfortable around them. They had a routine of sorts. She took care of the house and garden. They handled the farm and all the mechanical stuff. She usually gathered eggs in the morning, but if she was running behind, one of them gathered them for her.

There wasn't anything they wouldn't do for her. She often found herself watching them when they worked without their shirts. They were truly magnificent to look at. Muscles rippled across their chests and backs. How she had been so lucky to have chosen their trailer to stow away in, she would never know. She thanked God each night.

Then there was the sex. No, it wasn't just sex, but loving. They always pleasured her before taking their own. Sometimes they were tender and careful. But other times, they were wild and rough. She liked it both ways, and never complained. Sometimes, she would grab one of them and go to her knees to suck them off. They always praised her and thanked her for caring about them. She couldn't seem to get enough of them, and they of her.

But always in the back of her mind was the fact that they basically owned her. She knew it wasn't their fault, but just the way things were. Still, it felt suffocating to know that she couldn't go anywhere alone for fear that someone would snatch her.

If they noticed her occasional quiet spells, they didn't comment on them. They probably figured it was just hormones. She sighed and checked the corn. When she got to the end of the row, she looked out over the field of wildflowers behind it, and noticed the edge of the woods in the back had what looked like briars. Could there be blackberries among the briars?

Heather hurried through the field and checked the briars to find that there were. She eagerly began filling her bucket with the ripe berries. Time passed and she realized it was growing dark. She would have to hurry to get back to the house in time to start supper. She realized she'd worked her way much farther than she had planned.

She hurried back along the woods until she reached the spot behind the corn.

She had just emerged from the garden when Brandon exploded from the house, his face much like a thundercloud.

"Where in the hell have you been? We've been frantic looking for you." He grabbed her by the arm and pulled her into the house.

"Brandon, you're hurting me."

"I'm going to do more than that. I'm going to turn you over my knee and spank your ass until it turns a rosy red!"

Bolton slammed into the kitchen, looking as frantic as his brother looked angry.

"Where have you been?"

Tears stung her eyes. "I was picking blackberries for pies. I didn't realize you would worry about me. I was just along the woods' edge."

"You don't ever go anywhere without one of us knowing where you are. Better yet, you don't go anywhere without one of us being with you." Brandon began unfastening her jeans and jerked them down to her knees along with her underwear.

"No, don't hit me please, Brandon, don't hit me." She cowered trying to pull away from him.

Brandon cursed and turned away after letting her go.

"Go upstairs, Heather. Now!"

Heather was crying even before he pushed her away.

She jerked up her jeans and ran up the stairs. She could hear the two men arguing below as she threw herself on the bed and wept. She felt even more a prisoner than she had before. It had reminded her that they owned her. She was a possession, not a wife or lover so much as their property.

He wouldn't have really hurt her. She realized that now, but for a moment, she'd been back at the brothel and panicked. What did bother her was that she couldn't do anything without one of them there to watch her. She felt like a possession more than a human being sometimes.

She heard footsteps on the stairs and knew it would be Bolton. The bed dipped and he laid a hand on her back and rubbed light circles around it in a soothing motion.

"Heather? Are you okay?"

She just sniffed and refused to answer him.

"Honey, Brandon was scared to death someone had snatched you. I was scared to death."

He sighed and smoothed her hair from her face.

"Don't be mad at him, Heather."

"I'm nothing to either of you but a piece of your property. You don't really care about me. You just want to protect what you own." She felt the tears begin anew.

"That's not true." Brandon had come upstairs now. "You mean more to us than that."

"It doesn't feel that way. I'm not supposed to go anywhere or get out of your sight. I don't feel like I'm really part of you."

"Don't blame us for how things are. We can't help it that the world is like it is. If you get out of our sight, anyone can take you, and we couldn't do a damn thing about it. We would have to fight to get you back and there would be no guarantee we would ever find you," Brandon said.

She heard him spew a string of curses before he stomped back down the stairs. She heard the front door slam.

"You don't really believe all that, do you, Heather?" Bolton asked.

"I can't help how I feel. You treat me kind and give me what I need to take care of the house, but you are always telling me don't do this and don't go there. You keep reminding me that I'm not a person because I can't think or do anything on my own. It hurts, Bolton. I want this to be home to me, too. It doesn't feel like my home. Sometimes it feels like a prison."

How could she tell them that all she needed to feel a part of them was for them to tell her they loved her and needed her? She shouldn't have to tell them. They should want to tell her that. The fact that they hadn't only proved that they didn't, as far as she was concerned.

Bolton sighed and got up from the bed. He seemed to hesitate, then turned and walked away as well. She felt truly alone now. After several minutes of feeling sorry for herself, she got up and rinsed off the ravages of her crying jag and went back downstairs to do something for supper. It was her job, after all. She saw the berries sitting where she'd dropped them and picked the bucket up, tempted to dump them in the trash.

An hour later, she had supper ready, but neither of the men showed up to eat. After another hour, she fixed them a plate each and left them on the stove, and went to bed.

Chapter Four

The next morning she awoke with the knowledge that they hadn't come to bed during the night. She looked at the clock now sitting by the bed to find it was only five in the morning. She hurriedly dressed and tiptoed down stairs to start their coffee and breakfast. She figured they had slept in their old rooms. She hated that, but it was their prerogative.

An hour later, they clomped down the stairs and entered the kitchen. No one spoke. She served them their breakfast as usual with their coffee, but didn't sit down to eat with them. She didn't have a stomach for anything. When they had finished eating, they got up and walked to the door and left her in the kitchen. She felt a tear slip from her eyes, but she refused to let them take over.

She set up the kitchen to put up the blackberries as jelly. When lunchtime came and they didn't return, she took their sandwiches out to the field where they were cutting hay to put up for the winter. She didn't see them, so she called out. After a while, Bolton came up from the field. He looked at her with such sadness she wanted to hug him, but knew it wouldn't be welcomed. She handed him the sandwiches and turned around to walk back to the house.

"Thanks."

She turned around and smiled before heading back to the house. After that, things returned to normal for the most part. There was a wedge between them still, though, and she knew she was responsible for it. She didn't know how to fix it, and wasn't sure it was hers to fix.

One evening, Brandon announced they were going to Skylineto salvage again. He reminded her she needed more boots, and they needed to find her a coat for the winter coming up. He carefully laid out the rules to her. She was to stay with one of them at all times, and never go outside of one of the buildings alone.

"Do you understand why, Heather?"

"Yes. The wolves, and someone might snatch me," she answered in a dull voice. She hated having them remind her of that.

"Okay. We'll leave at dawn to make the most of the time we have. It gets dark earlier now," Brandon said.

They went to bed earlier as well, so that when it was time to get up, they had been rested. They were on the road before the sun was up. Bolton put his arm around her in the truck and hugged her.

"We'll find you some boots, and a coat, and some girly stuff."

"I don't need girly stuff. I don't have anywhere to wear it. We need to stick to useful stuff like soap and shampoo."

"Maybe I'd like to see you in some pretty things sometime," he told her.

"You're talking about lingerie?" She should have known.

"That would be nice, but maybe a pretty dress, too."

"If she doesn't want to wear it, don't make her, Bolton."

She noticed that Brandon gripped the wheel until his knuckles turned white. Did he not want her to dress sexy? Why? Maybe he was tired of her now. He still had sex with her and they still pleasured her, but he didn't cuddle with her as he had before. It hurt. She supposed she'd screwed everything up by being honest about her feelings.

When they arrived at Skyline, they headed for the Walmart first. Brandon pulled right up at the doors in the back. The three of them climbed out of the cab of the truck and carefully made their way inside. She let them lead her through the back into the main part of the building.

"Okay, Heather, grab a cart and go to the shoes first. Then go after whatever else you need or you think we need. We're going to be looking for some supplies in the automotive and hunting gear." Brandon pointed her to the cart they'd used last time.

She found three pair of boots that fit, and grabbed heavy socks as well as all the thermals and warm-ups that would fit her. Then she headed back to the pharmacy area and loaded up on shampoo, deodorant, and other supplies. She searched for a coat, but could only find jackets. She wandered through the lingerie and picked out a few things. There wasn't much to choose from in that department.

Bolton found her looking through the canning supplies. She had loaded another cart full of them and was struggling to pull one cart while she pushed another one.

"I've got this one. I'm glad you remembered the canning supplies. I had forgotten about them."

If he noticed the underwear she'd picked out, he didn't say anything. They made their way back to the double doors leading to the outside.

"Where is Brandon?"

"He's already out loading up what we found."

They eased through the back and loaded everything into the tubs they'd put there for that purpose. Then Brandon appeared and helped Bolton carry them to the truck. They left her in the back of the building to wait on them. The dark closed in around her, and she was tempted to slip out and get into the truck, but they'd been very clear she was to wait in the building. Finally, Bolton came for her.

"Remember, don't run. Walk slowly to the truck and climb in. We have company."

"Oh, my, God. There are wolves out there?"

"Just trust me and walk slowly to the truck."

Heather nodded and followed him outside. He grabbed her off the landing and stood her on her feet. They slowly walked to the truck and climbed in. The wolves had just watched them. She couldn't stop shivering.

"You okay?" Brandon asked.

"Yeah, they just scare me."

"Did you find a coat?" Bolton asked.

"No. I did find boots though, and I got thermal underwear."

Brandon maneuvered them around the deserted town until he pulled into a sporting goods parking lot. He pulled up close to the door.

"I've never been here, but they are bound to have coats here. Won't hurt for all of us to have extras," Brandon said. "Heather, stay in the truck until we get the doors open. Then one of us will come back after you."

She nodded and watched them climb out of the truck and make their way toward the front of the store. They used a crowbar to pry the door open. Then they checked inside before Bolton came back to get her.

"Remember. Walk, don't run. I don't see anything around us, but they're probably just hiding."

Heather followed Bolton and walked into the store. It was dark inside toward the back because there were no windows. Brandon appeared with a large flashlight that actually worked.

"Looks like all the coats are in the back. Bolton, I have her. You go get all the guns and ammunition and load them up."

Brandon took her to the back of the store where she tried on coats until she had three that fit. Then she grabbed thermals, figuring she couldn't have too many of them.

"Grab gloves, and a hat or two as well." Brandon pointed them out to her with the flashlight.

They backtracked to the front, and Brandon took everything from her to the truck. Then he helped Bolton finish gathering all the guns and ammunition. Heather saw the knives in the case and waited for one of them to come back in. Brandon and Bolton both walked back in for one last look.

"Can I have a knife out of that case over there? It could come in handy."

The brothers looked at each other and shrugged. Brandon ushered her over to the case and let her pick out two. They each got a couple as well.

"Better load up and grab a few batteries and get on the road. I don't want to be too late getting back," Brandon said.

After they loaded up on batteries out of an Auto Shack, they turned toward home. Heather realized she had thought of it as home. Maybe it was, and she was being silly about needing them to want her for more than just the physical part of a relationship. Maybe she'd just caused an unnecessary rift between them.

As soon as they drove up, they began unloading. Heather did her share, but they stopped her from unloading the guns, ammunition, and batteries.

"Go and put up your new clothes. We have the rest of this." Bolton turned her in the direction of the house.

Secretly, she was glad. She hadn't wanted to deal with the guns and stuff. She didn't much like them. Instead, she put away her things, fingering the silky underwear and wondering when she would feel up to wearing it for them. Maybe she would feel more like it later in the week. She heard the men downstairs, and waited on them to lock up and come upstairs. She needed them tonight and hoped they wanted her as well.

They took their shower together, and when she went to her knees in the shower to suck them both, they smiled down at her. She took turns sucking each cock deep in her throat until she could swallow around them. She licked up and down them like lollipops, and nipped the undersides of each of them until they were beginning to pant. When she fondled their balls, she could feel them draw up. She loved being able to manipulate their pleasure. It made her feel in control for once.

Brandon held her head still as he pumped in and out of her mouth, then Bolton took over and did the same thing. When they pulled out she whimpered, wanting to swallow their cum. Instead they each pumped their cocks and shot streams of cum along her breasts, then rubbed it in. For some reason, they liked to mark her, and it was one more reason she felt more like a possession, but she would never again say anything about it.

They gently cleaned her up and dried her off. When they began to play with her, she stopped them, saying she really wanted to snuggle. She'd lost the mood in the shower. Bolton pulled her into his arms and laid her across his chest. Brandon, though, just rested a hand on her ass and fell asleep. It hurt, but she was the cause of it. Maybe one day he would want the intimacy again. She prayed so, because it was killing her.

* * * *

Bolton spent more time around Heather, hoping to show her how much he cared about her. He had even told her he cared, but he was afraid it wasn't enough. Though she assured him she was fine and was happy, he still felt there was a part of her that wasn't. He knew that Brandon's behavior was a part of the problem, but he couldn't get through to his brother that he was making things worse.

Autumn turned to winter, and the first snow of the season descended on them. It was only a foot of snow, but Heather played in it like a child. Bolton even saw Brandon smile a couple of times at her antics. When she made snow angels, he fussed at her that she would end up sick if she got too wet. She just stuck her tongue out at him and continued. He stomped off and didn't return until suppertime. It hurt Heather's feelings. He could tell by the tremble to her bottom lip. Bolton didn't know what to do about his brother's attitude.

* * * *

The snow began to melt and turn the yard around them into mud. She fussed about cleaning mud up off the floor all the time. Soon they were shucking their boots at the back door. Bolton seemed amused by it, but Brandon growled and stomped through the house. Bolton had gone so far as to call him a spoiled brat. It hadn't gone over well.

"I need to go out and pull some greens for supper tonight. Do you want to go with me?" Heather asked.

"Naw, I'm staying in where it's warm. I'll watch you from inside. Don't be out too long. It's cold."

"I won't."

She pulled on her coat, hat, and gloves, and grabbed a dishpan. Then walked out the back to the garden and pulled what she needed for a meal. As she turned to go back in, someone grabbed at her. She thought at first it was one of the brothers, but his smell hit her. She screamed and tried to kick out at the man. He covered her mouth with his hand and she bit him. He backhanded her and tried to throw her over his shoulder, but she hit him over the head with the dishpan and screamed for Bolton.

The next thing she knew, Bolton and Brandon both were on the man, pulling him off her.

"In the house, now," Brandon yelled.

Heather ran for the house and slammed the door, locking it as well. She peered out the window to let the boys in as soon as they came up on the porch.

"What the hell happened?" Brandon demanded.

"I went out to gather some greens for supper, and he came up behind me." Tears streamed down her face.

"I've told you not to go anywhere by yourself."

"Don't fuss at her. I told her she could go out by herself. I was watching her, but I turned away long enough to get a cup of coffee. When I came back she was screaming. It's my fault." Bolton slammed his hand against the door.

"Where did the man go?"

"He escaped out into the woods. I didn't want to chase after him in case there was anyone else snooping around." Brandon ran a hand through his hair. "Fuck, look at your face. The bastard hit you."

Heather touched her face and winced. She was sure it was red, and would be blue by the morning.

"I'm sorry, Brandon."

"Hell, it's not your fault. Fuck!" Brandon grabbed a cloth and wet in with the cool water from the sink. He handed it to her. "Put it on your face, maybe it will keep the swelling down some."

Bolton wrapped his arms around her and led her to the other room, where he tugged her down into his lap. Brandon stomped back outside. Heather couldn't stop the tears. Whether they were from the fright and the pain of her face, or because Brandon had left her, she didn't know. All she knew was that they were growing farther and farther apart. It was breaking her heart. She knew she loved them both, and Brandon's withdrawal hurt.

They still had sex, but he wasn't in on it quite as much. She got the feeling he wasn't as pleased with her as before, and she didn't understand why. She tried hard to please him, but it didn't seem to be enough.

"Hey, honey. You need to calm down. It's over with now. We aren't going to let anyone hurt you again." Bolton held her close and kissed her temple, avoiding her bruised face.

"Why doesn't he like me anymore, Bolton?"

"He does like you. He just has a lot of stress right now. The weather is going to get worse before it gets better. It gets tough out here in the winter once the snow sets in."

"That's not all it is. He doesn't want me sexually like he used to. It hurts, Bolton."

"I know, honey. Give it some time. He'll come around."

* * * *

Brandon stomped out into the backyard where the guy had disappeared. He'd almost gotten her. If they'd been much later, he might have made it. He felt like a failure. He hadn't been able to protect her like he'd promised. It wasn't right that they had to worry, and she had to be watched like a hawk. No wonder she felt like a piece of meat being pulled along in every direction. She deserved better than that. She'd called herself a possession. She was much more than that. She was his life. He could finally admit to himself that he loved her. She would never believe it if he told her. She felt like he was the one keeping her captive. Well, she could think that way, and latch on to Bolton as her friend.

He sighed and ran a hand through his hair. They deserved each other. Maybe he needed to pull back all the way and let them bond. He would help protect her, but he wouldn't put pressure on her for sex. He was sure she felt like he was just using her.

The idea of letting her go stung, and nearly took his breath away. How could he live with them like that? If it weren't safer for all three of them to be together in one bedroom, he'd go back to sleeping in his old room. Even with the locks on the door, a thief would have no trouble breaking in. Especially if he knew they had a female.

Taking a deep breath of the fresh air to help clear his head, Brandon turned and walked back inside. He found Bolton and Heather curled up on the couch, fast asleep. He would let them sleep and fix a sandwich, then wake them up to go to bed. They both needed the rest. He and Bolton had been working hard for the last few weeks trying to get things ready for the when the heavier snow arrived.

He sat over in the chair opposite the couch and just watched them sleep. Heather had a dainty little snore that he found sweet. Bolton's wasn't. He smiled. His brother loved her as deeply as he did. It didn't bother him that Bolton loved her. It bothered him that she didn't trust him.

An hour later, he went over and shook Bolton awake.

"What?" He started to get up and seemed to realize he had Heather in his arms.

"You might want to think about getting her to bed. It's getting late."

"Yeah, sure. Don't go anywhere. I'll be right back down. We need to talk, Brandon."

Brandon just grunted and settled back in the chair. No doubt it would be another lecture about making Heather sad. It had been the same one over and over the last few weeks.

Bolton eased down the stairs and joined him back in the living room. He didn't look happy.

"Her face is going to be black and blue tomorrow. I shouldn't have taken my eyes off of her even for a second."

"She shouldn't have to be watched like that. It's fucking wrong," Brandon told him.

"Look, Brandon. I don't know what is going on with you, but you've got to stop alienating her. She's hurting. She thinks you don't like her anymore, and that she can't please you in bed anymore."

"That's bullshit. She's the most responsive woman I've ever had."

"Show her that. Tell her that. Do something besides rolling over and going to sleep."

"She doesn't want me to hold her, Bolton, she wants you. She thinks I just look at her as a possession. I can't stand that she feels that way, but nothing I've said has changed her mind." Brandon stood up and crossed to the fireplace. The embers were banked for a fire in the morning.

"Have you told her how much you care about her? She loves you, man."

"No she doesn't, she hates me, and I can't take much more of being around her and not being able to believe she sees me as more than her captor. I'm going to bed." He turned and walked up the stairs, leaving Bolton behind him to stew over what he'd said. He hoped Heather was asleep when he made it to bed.

Chapter Five

Several days went by, and Heather redoubled her efforts to capture Brandon's attention. He seemed to relax around her a little more and she reveled in it. A new snow began to fall, causing the men to be outside more and more tending to the animals. She missed them being around the house. She worked hard to keep hot food for them and plenty of wood in the fireplace so it would be warm when they got inside.

They seemed to appreciate it. At night, they made love. It was how she preferred to think about it. Just having sex made her feel dirty and cheap. Brandon joined them more often, and she began to think he was coming around.

One night, she climbed into bed and surprised Bolton by taking his rock-hard cock into her mouth. She licked up and down the silky shaft, paying special attention to the underside of the cap. She nibbled her way around it, then ran her tongue over the slit for a drop of cum. He hissed out a breath and grabbed at her head. She knew she was getting to him.

She felt Brandon behind her and smiled around Bolton's dick. He was going to fuck her. She couldn't help but hum in happiness around Bolton's cock. He moaned at the vibrations she caused to tingle along his cock. She sucked hard at the mushroom cap, then swallowed down his massive stalk.

Just then, Brandon licked up her slit, causing her to groan around the dick in her mouth.

"Fuck, that feels so damn good," Bolton managed to get out in a strained voice.

Brandon entered her with two fingers. He spread her to prepare her for his monster of a cock. When he positioned his dick at her entrance and pushed inward, Heather moaned her approval. He began a slow, steady rhythm that frustrated her. She wanted more, but when she tried to push back, he slapped her ass and told her to be still.

Bolton chuckled. In retaliation, she sucked him all the way to the back of her throat, then swallowed. He tangled his fingers in her hair and began to fuck her mouth in short, shallow pumps.

Brandon circled her back hole with something cold, then pushed in. She managed not to cry out, but it stung.

"Push out against my finger, Heather. It won't hurt as bad. I want to prepare you to take my cock so we can take you at the same time."

Heather wanted that desperately. She pushed out and his thumb popped inside past her tight ring. He slowly pushed farther in and pulled out, only to do it again and again. She found that it began to feel good. Nerves she hadn't known existed came alive and tingled.

Brandon pulled out his thumb and pushed in two fingers now. It stung again, but she pushed out and let them enter her. He scissored them back and forth, spreading her ass in the process. He continued to pummel her pussy with his cock, matching the rhythm with his fingers.

She began to suck harder on Bolton before she couldn't concentrate on him. She wrapped her hand around him and worked his dick as she sucked. It wasn't long before he began grunting, and she knew he was about to come. She redoubled her effort, and was soon rewarded with streams of cum deep in her throat. She hummed her approval and licked him clean.

With Bolton taken care of, Brandon began pounding into her from behind. She growled, and began to meet him thrust for thrust. The fingers in her ass were wonderful. She never would have believed it. They touched nerve endings she'd never felt before and made her feel full. How would she feel with his massive cock inside her ass? Could she even take him? God, she would do anything for him.

He reached around at that time and tapped at her clit, sending her into spasm after spasm of climax like she'd never felt before. She felt him still behind her, and warm streams of his cum filled her pussy. He collapsed on top of her for a few seconds, breathing hard. Then he pulled out and left her there to go to the bathroom. He came back with a bath cloth and cleaned her up, then climbed into bed and patted her on the arm before turning over and going to sleep.

* * * *

Bolton ground his teeth at the way Brandon left her like that. He pulled her into his arms and kissed along her neck and cheek.

"Shh. I've got you, Heather."

She didn't make a sound, but he could feel the silent sobs from her tiny body. It was then that he realized she had lost weight again. Fuck, Brandon and his stubborn self. He lulled her into sleep, then thought about what to do. He was sick of Brandon treating her like a whore. As far as he was concerned, that was what he was doing. They were brothers, but he almost hated him in that moment.

He managed to sleep for several hours, but he dreamed of them as a family with everything working like it was supposed to. They made love together, and Brandon treated her like the precious gift she was to them. When he woke up several hours later, he couldn't go back to sleep.

Trying not to wake anyone up, he slid out of bed and grabbed his clothes. He slipped downstairs and dressed. It was nearly five, so it would be time to get up in a couple of hours, anyway. He would get a head start on the chores.

Heather usually got the eggs and milked the cow. He'd get all of that done after he made a pot of coffee. It wasn't long before he heard footsteps on the stairs, and knew they were Brandon's by the heavy tread. He steeled himself not to light into him when he walked into the kitchen.

"What are you doing up so early?" his brother asked.

"Couldn't sleep."

"What are you planning to do?"

"Gather the eggs and milk the cow so Heather doesn't have to get out in the cold this morning." Bolton poured a cup of coffee as soon as the pot was full.

Brandon took down a cup and helped himself as well. He didn't say anything, so Bolton kept quiet as well. The rift between them was palpable, but he wasn't going to be the one to bring it up. After a few minutes, he finished his coffee and grabbed the buckets and left his brother standing at the kitchen counter.

Maybe he should suggest that Brandon move back into his room and stay away from Heather altogether. It would hurt her at first, but she would get used to it, and it would put a stop to the constant upheaval she was going through daily. He wasn't sure he could do it, though. Should he discuss it with Heather first? He didn't have the answer to that.

Once he finished the chores, he took the milk and eggs back inside and wrote out a note to let Heather know he'd already done everything so she wouldn't look for the buckets. Then he went back outside to join Brandon feeding the cattle. They had to keep hay out in the field for them to eat in the cold. They had brought them closer to the house to offer some protection from the harsh winds.

Bolton found Brandon already out in the field spreading hay. He joined him, and they worked in silence for nearly an hour in the harsh cold. Then Brandon motioned for him to follow him farther out in the field.

"Look what I found." He pointed to some tracks in the snow.

"Fuck, is that a wolf?" Bolton squatted to get a better look.

"Yep. It's the only set I've found so far, but it doesn't mean there aren't more. We're going to have to watch for it. It will be going after the cows and the chickens."

"Maybe we should hunt for it." Bolton stood back up.

"I figure so as well. We'll wait and see if we find anymore tracks. It might just be passing through. They hunt in packs. It might be looking for a pack to join."

"I was thinking of going deer hunting tomorrow morning. I can keep a lookout while I'm out," Bolton said.

"Good idea. Fresh deer meat would be good. Um, Heather has lost some weight."

"Yeah and you should know why." Bolton walked off, fuming.

He walked back to the house and when he opened the door, he found Heather cooking breakfast. She turned and smiled.

"You are out early. Thanks for doing my chores. I appreciate it."

"Woke up early, so I decided to get a head start. Breakfast smells great."

"Brandon coming in?" She asked it casually without looking at him.

"Should be on in, in a few minutes. He was checking the horses."

She had breakfast on the table before Brandon finally walked through the door. He peeled out of his coat, scarf, and gloves and hung his hat on the peg.

"Something smells good."

"I cooked some of the deer sausage this morning. I figured you could do with some extra protein being out in the cold."

"Thanks." Brandon sat down and filled his dish. Then he looked over at her plate and frowned. "You need more than that."

"I nibbled while I was cooking. I'm already nearly full."

Bolton caught his attention and shook his head. Brandon frowned at him, but didn't say anything more about her needing to eat more. Bolton planned on bringing it up later. He didn't want Brandon upsetting her. He had already done enough harm.

When they were finished, they started bundling up to go back out in the cold. Heather walked over to him and gave him a loud smack on the lips, then turned to Brandon and pulled his head down for a kiss. He let her, but he didn't return it. She let go of him and backed up a step.

"Um, be careful out there." She turned and began gathering up the plates.

Bolton was about ready to beat the living hell out of his brother now.

* * * *

Heather kept busy in the house through most of the winter. The men spent a lot of time outside in the harsh weather. Sometimes she felt so alone during the day. Then, when they were back inside, she was happy again. If only she could do more outside. It wouldn't be so bad then. Part of the loneliness stemmed from the fact that Brandon still seemed so distant.

He continued to fuck her with Bolton at least, but never in any position other than behind her. He kept stretching her ass, but he never penetrated her with his cock. She'd all but begged him to. Telling him she wanted to feel him inside her. Still, he resisted that last piece of intimacy. It hurt, but she was thankful for what she had. She could be back in the brothel servicing every man that came through.

When the men came in tonight, she was going to give Brandon a blow job. She hadn't done that in a while. Surely he wouldn't stop her from doing that. She'd catch him when he came out of the shower and was drying off. He'd not be able to resist her that way. She had it all planned out.

Sure enough, when he walked out of the shower, he was still toweling off. She grabbed the towel from him and dropped it on the floor to kneel in front of him.

"Heather, what are you doing?"

"What does it look like?" She took his semihard cock in her hand. "I'm having cock for dessert."

She sucked the bulbous head into her mouth as hard as she could and was rewarded with a "Holy crap."

"You don't have to do this, Heather," he said through gritted teeth.

"I want to." She redoubled her effort to get him hard. He wasn't responding.

Brandon grabbed her head and groaned. "Heather, I don't think I can right now."

She wouldn't give up. She fondled his balls, but he remained only semierect. She stopped and stared up at him with tears in her eyes.

"Why not?"

"I'm just really tired tonight, Heather. It's not you. Come on." He reached down and pulled her up. "Let's go to bed."

He picked her up and carried her to bed, and actually wrapped an arm over her. She sighed around the tears. It wasn't any time until he began snoring. When Bolton came to bed later, he looked at her and lifted an eyebrow. She shook her head and closed her eyes. Sleep wouldn't come. She heard Brandon sigh and roll over, leaving her without the comfort of his arm across her belly. She swallowed and tried to fall asleep, but nothing she did worked.

Finally, she climbed out of bed sliding to the foot of the bed to keep from waking the men. Then she gathered her clothes and dressed in the bathroom. She hurried down the stairs and found that it was four in the morning. She added wood to the fireplace and stirred the embers to start the fire so she wouldn't be cold. Then she curled up on the couch with a blanket around her.

Two hours later, she got up and set up the coffee. Then she fixed a cup of hot chocolate for herself. The men came downstairs a few minutes later dressed for the cold with thermals and long-sleeve shirts. They immediately headed for the coffee.

"Probably won't be out as long today," Bolton told her. "With the snow slowly melting, there isn't as much to do."

"Good. It will be good to have you inside. I miss you when you're gone."

Bolton pulled her into his arms and kissed her hungrily. She returned the kiss and enjoyed the warmth of his body against hers. She wished Brandon would do the same thing, but he rarely kissed her anymore.

"I'm going out to get the eggs and milk. I'll be back in to start breakfast in a few minutes."

"Be careful out there," Brandon said.

"I'll watch her," Bolton said and pulled on his coat as she did.

"I'll be okay, Bolton. You don't have to come out and watch me."

"I like watching you, though," he confessed with a smile.

She shrugged and winked at him then, grabbed her buckets and headed out into the snow, paying close attention to how she stepped. She didn't want to fall in the frozen snow if she could help it.

The chickens raised a fuss as they always did when she opened the coop. They refused to come out, and she spent ten minutes avoiding pecking birds as she emptied their nests. Then she poured grain on the floor, and in the trough at the back of the coop. When she closed the coop behind her, Bolton took the bucket of eggs.

"I'll take these in for you and be right back out."

"I'll be safe in the barn, silly."

"Like I said. I like to watch you." He turned and walked toward the house.

Heather smiled and opened the barn door to the moos of their Jersey cow. She pulled off her gloves and sat down to milk her. It always took a few tries before she got it right, and was soon pulling milk without trouble. The cow turned her head and mooed at her again.

"Sorry. I wore gloves to keep my hands as warm as possible."

"You should have let me warm them up for you first," Bolton said as he walked into the barn.

"You startled me. Now I'm out of rhythm."

He laughed and knelt behind her, and put his hands over hers and helped her start back. He let go of her hands and pulled her hair away from her shoulder, then bent down to suck at her neck.

Heather shivered and giggled. He was in a mood. She liked it when he got in one of those moods, but they were out in the barn, in the cold. Once she'd finished milking the cow, she stood up and bent to get the bucket. He stopped her and backed her over to an empty stall where they kept the extra horse blankets.

"I want you just like this," he said.

He began unfastening her jeans. He pushed them down, then turned her around to the blankets and had her get on all fours. She looked over her shoulder and watched him unfasten his jeans and push them to his knees. He pushed two fingers inside of her already-weeping pussy and made sure she was ready for him. Then he plunged inside of her as far as he could make it in one push.

Heather bit her hand to keep from screaming out. The pressure was so good. He backed out and plunged again until he was all the way inside of her hot cunt.

"Fuck, you are so tight, Heather." He continued to pummel her as he reached around and played with her clit. "Come for me, baby. I can't last long in your tight pussy."

Heather could feel the gathering electrical current pulsing in her clit as he manipulated it. Fire flowed through her veins as the heat gathered inside her cunt. He groaned and pinched her clit. It was all it took to send her over the edge. She bit her hand and groaned as she felt Bolton shoot his cum deep inside of her.

He huffed, trying to catch his breath. He slowly stood up and helped her to stand as well. They fastened their clothes and straightened them before looking at each other and laughing. She felt like she'd snuck away from school to have a quickie behind the bleachers. Bolton picked up the bucket of milk and they carefully negotiated the icy snow back to the house.

Brandon was nowhere to be seen. There was tomato gravy and biscuits on the stove. Heather felt guilty then. She hadn't fixed his breakfast before he'd gone out in the snow to take care of the animals. Then she wondered if he'd heard them and knew what they'd been doing. She grimaced. What if he did? It wasn't like he wanted to do anything with her. She put away the eggs and skimmed the milk before putting it away. She would fix soup for lunch and makesandwiches as well.

When the men came in later, she had everything ready for them. They ate, then retired to the living room to rest. She had just put on a new log, so the room was nice and toasty. She went to Brandon and curled up in his lap where he sat in one of the lounge chairs. He didn't push her out, but he didn't hug her, either. She refused to give up on him. Several hours later, he picked her up and sat her on the couch.

"Time to check the cows again."

Bolton stood up and stretched. He walked over to Heather and kissed her before following Brandon into the kitchen to bundle up and head outside. She didn't bother getting up to watch them this time. She continued sitting on the couch thinking about life and her need to please Brandon despite his obvious resistance. He'd wanted her once.What was different now?

She thought back and realized it had all started after she'd first gotten there and argued that she was just a possession to them. Had he gotten so mad at her for that, that he no longer wanted her? She hated to think it was all her fault. Why was he holding a grudge when Bolton wasn't?

Heather was still thinking about it when the men got back for the night. She hadlet the fire die down, and realized she was cold. She hurried to add a log, then went to serve them the last of the soup and leftover biscuits from breakfast.

She hugged them both and told them she was going to call it a night and go to bed early.

"You okay, Heather?" Bolton asked.

"I'm fine, just tired today. I'll see you when you come to bed."
She kissed him and headed upstairs.

She didn't miss the fact that Brandon avoided her kiss by getting
up to go into the kitchen. She tried not to dwell on it, but couldn't
help that it hurt just the same. She vowed to get up early enough to
join him in the shower and help him bathe. He couldn't very well
push her out. At least she hoped not.

Chapter Six

Heather woke up and noticed that both men were already up. Damn, had she missed Brandon? She listened and realized someone was in the shower. She climbed out of bed and slipped into the bathroom. Whoever it was would get her attentions this morning.

She turned the corner to walk into the shower, and stopped dead. Brandon was in the shower with one hand wrapped around his jutting cock and the other squeezing his balls, jacking off. She must have made a sound, because he turned and looked at her.

"Fuck, Heather."

"You can't fuck me but you can jack off. That's why you never feel like fucking me. You've jacked off in the shower thinking of someone else. Hell, fine. Think about someone else, but I'm not even a poor substitute. I'm not worth fucking at all."

Brandon slapped the back of the shower stall. "It's not like that, Heather. You don't understand."

"Oh, I understand. I'm nothing to you except as a maid and working around the farm. I'm not even as good as a whore. Do you have any idea how badly you're hurting me?"

She ran out of the bathroom and pulled on her jeans without underwear, and her shirt without a bra or thermals. She swallowed back the tears and raced out of the bedroom as Brandon walked out of the bathroom with a towel around his waist.

"Heather, come back here. It's not what you think."

She passed Bolton on the stairs. He grabbed her arm.

"What's wrong?"

"Ask your fucking brother. I'm going to get the eggs and milk. It's about all I'm good for." She pulled her arm from his grasp and hurried down the stairs.

She donned her coat and scarf and gloves, and grabbed the buckets before slamming out of the house. Now the tears fell in great rivers. She could hardly see to find her way to the chicken coop. When she drew closer, she heard the birds screeching and flapping around inside. What in the hell was wrong with them? She threw open the door and the birds flew out, nearly blinding her.

"What the fuck?" Then something hit her and knocked her down.

It growled and she felt hot breath against her face. Oh, God! It was a wolf. She screamed and threw up her arms in self-defense. It latched onto her left arm and shook her. She screamed again. The wolf continued to gnaw at her. It shook her like a rag doll. Then Bolton was suddenly there, trying to pull the big animal off of her.

She heard Brandon from a long ways away telling Bolton to move. Then there was a shot, and another one. God, her arm hurt. It felt like a thousand knives were stabbing in her over and over. Bolton knelt by her, yelling at Brandon to help him. He picked her up, and the pain was too much for her. Heather passed out.

* * * *

Bolton rushed her in the house with Brandon right behind him. They ran up the stairs and laid her on the bed. She was white as a sheet. Brandon cursed and pulled a knife from the bedside table to cut the coat off of her. Thank God she had it on. It had taken most of the bites, but not all of them.

"There's so much blood, Brandon." Bolton pulled her boots off of her while his brother cut the coat off.

"Go get all the first aid supplies we have. Everything."

Brandon managed to get most of the sleeve off and found that she had multiple bite wounds up and down her arm. She had a few cuts on her side as well. He leaned in and sniffed. He didn't smell bowel, so he assumed nothing had been punctured. Hell, what could he have done if it had been punctured?

Don't borrow trouble. Concentrate on what you can do.

He grabbed a towel and wrapped her arm in it to help staunch the flow of blood. He squeezed. She didn't so much as flinch. She should be screaming in pain right then, but instead she lay as if dead.

Just as Bolton returned with a huge box of supplies, she began to shiver.

"Ah, hell. She's going into shock. Bolton, cover her up and put a pillow or two under her feet."

He hurried to stuff the blanket around her, and then elevated her feet like Brandon had said. Then he stood and watched as Brandon removed the towel to see how the bleeding was.

"Shit, Brandon, what can we do?"

"Calm down, for one thing. We've got to sew up these cuts, but we've got to clean them first. I think most of the bleeding has stopped." Brandon swallowed and prayed they could do this.

"Go get several hot, wet cloths and the hydrogen peroxide."

While Bolton was gone, he checked the wounds for debris but found none. Thank God for the snow. It had been clean, so all they had to worry about was the saliva and teeth from the wolf, which would be dirty enough.

"What do you want me to do with them?" Bolton asked.

"Pour the peroxide all over the wounds first. Then we have to clean them with the cloths."

Bolton poured the peroxide all over her arm. Brandon lifted it, and he poured it on the back side as well. Then they each took a bath cloth and cleaned at the wounds. Brandon made sure they got the ones on her abdomen as well. Once they had them as clean as he thought they could manage, he rummaged through the box and pulled out all the sutures they had.

"We've got to sew her up now, Bolton. We've sewed each other up, so we can do her. We need to hurry before she wakes up, because we don't have anything to deaden her arm."

"Brandon? I don't know if I can."

"Get hold of yourself, Bolton. You have to. I can't do it all. Start with the ones on her side."

Bolton got on the bed, and Brandon pulled up a chair to make sure he would be steady. Then he made the first stick of many.

He swallowed hard when she began to stir. He was only halfway through with her arm. Bolton was finished with her side, and had started on her arm with him.

"Oh, what are you doing to me? Please, don't do that anymore." Heather began to thrash on the bed.

"Hold her, Bolton. We have to finish this."

Bolton turned white, but he wrapped his arms around her and held her still, talking to her the entire time. He kept swallowing as if he were trying not to get sick.

Brandon ground his teeth and kept going, trying to shut out her screams. Finally, thankfully, she fainted. Bolton was crying. Brandon felt tears dripping from his own face. God, he had nearly killed her stitching her up. By the time he had finished, he'd broken out in a cold sweat and felt as if he was going to be sick.

"She's going to be okay, isn't she?" Bolton asked.

"If she doesn't get an infection, she will."

"I don't think the wolf was rabid. It wasn't foaming at the mouth. I think she got in the way of him getting to the chickens, and he attacked her." Bolton looked back at where she lay under piles of covers.

"I fucking should have gone after the damn thing when we found the prints." Brandon ran a bloody hand through his hair.

"We didn't find any other prints.There was no reason for us to think it was still around. It's no more your fault than it is mine," Bolton told him.

"If she hadn't found me in the shower jacking off, she wouldn't have run out there in the first place."

"You were doing what?" Bolton stared at him as if he'd grown a second head.

"I'm going to get rid of the wolf and salvage what we can of the chickens. You stay by her and keep her warm. If she wakes up, give her as much water as she'll drink."

"Don't you fucking walk away from this, Brandon."

"Leave it be for now, brother. We can fight about it later. Not while she's like this." He turned and stalked out of the room. He had to get away before he broke down.

He pulled on his coat and gloves and walked outside to breathe in the fresh air. The bite of cold helped to clear his head some, but not enough to stop the tears. He'd fucked up big time. After a few minutes standing in the freezing cold, he walked over to where the wolf lay in the snow and dragged its carcass over toward the woods. He would have to figure out a way to bury it. With the ground frozen, he wasn't sure he would be able to.

He returned to the barn and got a shovel, but soon gave up at digging in the frozen ground. Instead, he would have to drag the wolf as deep in the woods as he could, so that the smell of it decomposing come spring wouldn't reach them. He dragged the thing deep into the woods until he gave out and dropped it. Then he made his way back to where the bloody snow was, He took the shovel and covered it up. He didn't want the reminder every time he walked outside.

Most of the chickens were back in the coop. He gathered the eggs in his hat and fed them.Then shooed the remainder of them back in the coop and fastened the door closed. He would have to return with a fresh bucket to milk the cow. He resisted going upstairs to check on her. If he did, he might not come back down to take care of the cow.

What if she died? How could he go on knowing he'd caused it? He never thought she would find out what he'd been doing. It wasn't someone else he thought about when he jacked off, it was her. It was how he wanted her to be. Brandon wanted her to be happy and in love with them. She saw him as her jailer, and not as someone she could love. He wanted them to be a family, but she thought she was only a possession to him. Something he owned. Now she thought she wasn't even as good as a whore.

He broke down as he milked the cow, and sobbed like a child.

* * * *

Bolton sat in the chair next to the bed and watched her. He wiped his eyes with the sleeve of one arm, but they just teared up again. What in the hell had Brandon been thinking? Why would he use his own hand when they had Heather? It wasn't as if she didn't want to. More often than not, she had been the instigator when it came to sex. She'd pushed hard with Brandon, but he hadn't been interested. Why? Fuck! Everything was such a fucking mess.

Heather stirred and moaned. He immediately grabbed the bottle of Tylenol and shook out two. He lifted her head and tried to get her to swallow the pills.

"Come on, baby. The Tylenol will make you feel better. Swallow them and some water for me."

She choked, but managed to get the two pills down and several swallows of water. Thenshe turned her head and fell back into a restless sleep. Her arm was swollen already. Did that mean infection had already set in? He couldn't remember if their wounds had swollen when they had to get stitches.

Her face held a grimace, and she remained white as a sheet. He smoothed her hair back from her face, and realized there was blood matted in it as well. He got up and wet another bath cloth, and gently cleaned her face and the hair around it.

What was taking Brandon so long? He needed him. He didn't know what to do if she woke up, and he couldn't keep her still. He was so afraid of hurting her.

Bolton got up and straightened the bed, making sure the covers didn't bind her. Then he paced, unable to be still. His eyes never left her face. The minute she moved her head, he was back, talking to her. He whispered how much he loved her in her ear, and that she had to get well soon. Then he did something he hadn't done since they'd lost their family all those years ago. He prayed.

After what seemed like hours, her heard Brandon's steps on the stairs. He didn't come into the room, but walked farther down the hallway to his old room. Bolton heard the door close and wondered what he was doing. Why had he gone down there? Even if he needed to clean up, all his clothes were in here. At least he thought they were. He got up and checked the chest and the closet. Maybe they weren't. It looked like some were missing. What in the hell had his brother been thinking all these months?

Thirty minutes later, Brandon walked into the room in clean jeans and a long-sleeve shirt. He'd showered and changed clothes. Clothes that had not been in the room they shared with Heather.

"I'll watch her while you clean up. If she wakes up, she doesn't need to see you covered in blood." Brandon walked over to the other side of the room and looked out the window.

Bolton started to light into him, but noticed how red his eyes were. He'd been crying, and Brandon hadn't even cried when they'd buried their parents and little sister.

"She woke up about an hour ago, enough that I got two pain pills in her and a few sips of water. She's restless, but she hasn't woken again." Bolton didn't bother to hide the disgust in his voice. He was pissed, and didn't care if Brandon was hurting or not. He should be.

Brandon just nodded and continued to look out the window.

Bolton grabbed some fresh clothes and climbed into the shower. He didn't bother waiting on the water to warm up. He wanted to get back in the other room with Heather. He was so afraid she would wake, and he would miss it. He scrubbed all the dried blood from his body, then rinsed off. By the time he had dried off and was dressed, he was nearly out of breath. He opened the bathroom door to find Brandon sitting in the chair bent over near her ear, whispering something to her. He couldn't make out what it was.

He must have made some noise, because Brandon pulled back and stood up.

"You can sit with her while I cook something for us to eat."

"I'm not hungry. You go ahead if you can."

Brandon grabbed him by the arm and pulled him up close. "I'm not a bit fucking hungry, but we both have to eat and keep up our strength because we're going to be staying up with her around the clock, and still take care of the damn farm."

"Fine, fix something. I'll eat, and I'll take care of her while you take care of your farm." Bolton turned away.

Brandon didn't stop him this time. "Without this farm, we don't have food to feed her. I could give a rat's ass about the fucking farm, but we need it to take care of her. If it falls apart around us, we don't have any way to feed her or make her well."

Bolton turned around to agree with him, but his brother had already walked out of the room. He could hear his tread on the stairs. Damn, they didn't need to be fighting while Heather was hurt. They needed to both be taking care of her. As much as he wanted to rip Brandon a new asshole, he needed his brother's help to care for her.

A few minutes later, Heather began to moan and move her head back and forth. She still felt cool to him. He couldn't give her more pain medication yet. It was too soon. He lifted her again and urged her to drink some more water. She resisted at first, then took a sip. She began gulping the water as fast as he gave it to her. He didn't want her to get sick, so he pulled it back and waited to see if she acted like she wanted more. She relaxed and her head lolled to one side.

Brandon walked back into the room.

"She drink some water?" Brandon asked as Bolton settled her back in the bed.

"Yeah. About half the glass this time."

"I've got you a bowl of stew and some bread. It's the last of the loaf she cooked yesterday."

"Did you eat?" Bolton took the bowl and bread.

"Yeah, tasted like cardboard, and that ain't her cooking."

Bolton spooned some of the stew into his mouth and swallowed without really tasting it. He nodded toward the bed.

"Look at her arm. It's awful swollen. Is it supposed to do that?"

Brandon slipped between him and the bed and pulled back the cover to look at Heather's arm. It looked even larger to Bolton since the last time he'd looked at it.

"Yeah, it's pretty swollen. It's gonna swell some from all the trauma, but I'm afraid she's going to end up with an infection, too. It's too early to tell, though. We'll keep it clean and dry. I'm going to get a towel to put under it, and we'll keep the cover off of it. Grab a pillow and let's elevate it some, so maybe it won't throb when she wakes up." Brandon stood up and walked over to the bathroom, then returned a few seconds later with a towel.

Bolton sat aside his meal and helped him situate her arm on the pillow and towel. They folded the cover back away from it.

"Can't we get those bloody clothes off her?" Bolton asked.

"Not now. Let's wait until we see if she's going to run a fever, then we'll bathe her and changed her clothes."

"You think she's going to get sick, don't you?" Bolton sighed.

"Her arm is too puffy already."

"What can we do for her if she does get sick?"

"Keep her dry and comfortable and pray. It's about all we have to work with, Bolton."

Brandon started to walk away, but Bolton stopped him. "Why, Brandon?"

His brother didn't say anything for a long time. He didn't even turn back around to look at him. Finally his shoulders dropped and he hung his head.

"Because I was a fool. I wanted her to love me like she loves you, but all she sees me as is her keeper. She thinks I feel like I'm stuck with her, so I'm making the best of it."

"That isn't true, Brandon."

"I know that now, but before…" He didn't finish. Instead he drew in a deep breath and walked out of the room.

Bolton rubbed his hands over his face and sighed. The whole world was fucked up, and they were still screwing up their own little piece of it, as well.

Chapter Seven

Brandon and Bolton took turns sitting with her the rest of the day and into the night. Around four that morning, Brandon touched her forehead and found it burning up. She was spiking a fever. He cursed and grabbed the thermometer he'd found in the first aid kit and ran it along her forehead. It registered one hundred and five degrees.

"Bolton! Wake up." He pulled the covers off of her and began undressing her.

"What the fuck are you doing?" Bolton sat up in the bed and watched him in horror.

"She has one hundred and five temperature. We've got to get it down. Help me take her clothes off, and go get wet towels. We'll bathe her and see if that will bring it down."

Bolton disappeared into the bathroom. Brandon heard the water running. Then he was back with several cool, wet towels. They washed her down with them. Brandon placed one of them across her neck, and another across her forehead. After a few minutes, he took her temperature again, but it hadn't changed.

"Fuck! It's not working."

"What can we do?" Bolton had pulled on a pair of jeans now, and was struggling into his socks.

Brandon searched his mind for what they could do to break her fever. All he knew was to keep bathing her in cool water. He couldn't put her in a cold tub because of the wounds on her abdomen and arm. They couldn't get the stitches wet. Panic tightened his throat and lodged a rock in his chest.

"Go downstairs and get one of the washtubs. Bring back some more towels and we'll run cold water in it and keep bathing her with it. It's all I know to do right now."

By the sound of it, Bolton ran down the stairs. He'd be lucky if he didn't break his fool neck, Brandon thought. Shaking his head, he removed the drying towels and replaced them with wet ones again. Her fever was drying them out as fast as he replaced them.

When Bolton returned to the bedroom after filling the washtub with cold water, Brandon had him help hold her up so he could try and force more water down her. She fought it, but they managed to get a little more in her.

"Roll her over and let me bathe her back," Brandon told his brother.

After he had cleansed her back, they began laying cold, wet towels over her body, working through the rest of the early morning hours. At a quarter of seven, Bolton finished dressing and took his turn at doing the daily chores and tending to the animals. Brandon remained with Heather, sponging her down over and over. He was exhausted from lack of sleep, but he wasn't giving up.

Several hours later, Bolton returned and took over the job. Brandon stood up and stretched. He felt like death warmed over. Then he felt guilty for thinking that. He was healthy, and Heather was fighting for her life. He crawled up next to her in the bed and took her uninjured hand in his. Then he willed himself to sleep. He needed as much rest as he could manage, so he could stay up with her again that night and relieve Bolton.

He must have dozed at some point, because Bolton shook him awake.

"I need to check the cows and fix us something to eat."

"What time is it?"

"A little after noon." Bolton waited for him to shake himself awake and climb out of the bed. "I'll be back up in a few hours, and then we need to talk."

Brandon grimaced, but nodded. He was right. They needed to talk before Heather woke up. They needed to settle things before they had to face her. Dear God. Let them have to face her.

He checked Heather's temperature and found it was still 104. He didn't know what else they could do. He continued bathing her in the cold, wet towels and forcing Tylenol down her every four hours. All the time he was caring for her, he was thinking about how he should have been caring for her all along.

You were a fool, Brandon. She tried to let you know she cared about you over and over again, but your stupid fucking pride just wouldn't believe it.

Instead, he had felt sorry for himself because he believed she loved and cared about his brother, and only tolerated him. She had said that he was her keeper, her jailer. He believed she meant it. Maybe she had in the beginning. He'd been tough on her, but it was dangerous in the world today, and he was responsible for making sure she was safe. There was that word again, responsible.

Several hours later, Bolton returned with a grim expression on his face.

"What's wrong?"

"Nothing. Just trying to figure out how in the hell we ended up in this mess."

Brandon shook his head. "It's all my fault. I let my feelings get hurt and made a mountain out of a molehill."

"If you didn't love her, why did you keep fucking her at all? You could have said something to me. I would have talked to her, and it would have been all right, eventually."

"Because I do love her, dammit!" He ran a hand over his face. "I've loved her ever since she stepped out of the back of that trailer in Barter Town."

"I don't get it. If you love her, why did you pull away from her like you did?"

"Remember when we first got home with her? She said I didn't really care about her. That she was just a responsibility, and I was her jailer. She kept away from me after that, and nothing I did got her to warm up to me. I let it get to me and refused to let her under my skin, but she was already there."

"Why in the hell would you go and act like a fucking three-year-old?" Bolton demanded.

"Because I didn't believe she could love me and you, both."

"Now we might never know," Bolton said.

Brandon continued changing out the towels on Heather's neck and forehead.

"So you were jacking off in the shower and she caught you."

"I'd been trying to pull back, so you and she could maybe bond and be a couple. I honestly didn't think she could ever care about me like she did you. I felt like I was forced on her."

"She cared about you, Brandon. Hell, I think she even loved you." He hit the door facing with his hand. "And we're talking about her like she's gone or something."

"I can't get her fever down, Bolton. We're going to lose her if I don't get it to break."

"Maybe it would be better to soak her in the tub and just let the damn stitches get wet."

"I know. Hell, why didn't I think of it before?" He ran out of the room with Bolton calling after him.

"What?"

"Just a minute," Brandon called over his shoulder as he took the stairs two at a time.

He grabbed a box of freezer bags out of the pantry and opened the back door to scoop up snow and ice into each one of them. When he had four bags of ice, he closed the door and ran back up to the bedroom.

"What?" Bolton asked again.

"Here, take these and put them at her groin. Hold them there. I'm going to put these under her arms. I remember now, when you had the measles and ran such a high fever that mom did this to you to get the fever down."

They pressed the bags of icy snow at her pulse points where the blood would grow cooler as it passed by the bags of ice. Brandon went down again and replaced the thawed water with more ice bags two more times before her fever finally broke. Once it got down to a little over a hundred, Brandon stopped the ice treatments and they cleaned her up and dried her off.

It took both of them to dry her and change the sheets each time she sweated more of the fever off. They took turns with the animals and farm chores. Neither of them got much sleep, but she was doing better, and all Brandon could do was pray that the fever hadn't caused any brain damage. He knew that could happen, but hadn't mentioned it to Bolton.

On the third evening, Brandon was forcing more water down her when she opened her eyes for a few brief seconds. He was so excited he opened the window and called out to Bolton to come up quick. His poor brother nearly broke his neck running up the stairs.

"What is it?"

"She opened her eyes for a few seconds. She's coming around now."

"Ah, hell yes!" Bolton grabbed the chair and sat down to rub his knuckles across her cheek. She turned her head into it.

Brandon smiled for the first time in what felt like forever. Maybe it had been forever.

"Can you hear me, baby? Wake up for us, Heather. We miss you." Bolton brushed her hair away from her eyes and leaned in and kissed her lips.

She licked her lips and made an "mmm" sound. Her eyelids fluttered, but she didn't open her eyes again.

"She's waking up.It won't be long now," Bolton predicted with a wide smile creasing his face.

"What were you doing? I'll go finish it and you can sit up here with her for a while," Brandon offered.

"I was finished and coming in the house anyway. Don't go anywhere. She might wake up. She's going to want to see you."

"I'm probably the last person she's going to want to see."

"You're not pulling away until I hear her tell you she doesn't want anything to do with you. You're going to explain, just like you did to me, what you've been doing," Bolton argued.

Brandon shook his head, but sat on the edge of the bed and willed her eyes to open. He missed seeing their sky blue orbs with the twinkle in them when she was amused or up to something.

When they finally did, he breathed a sigh of relief.

* * * *

Heather felt as if her arm had been through a meat grinder. It didn't just ache. It hurt enough there were tears in her eyes. She moaned and opened her eyes to see what was wrong with her arm. Both brothers were there. Brandon sat on the edge of the bed near her knees and Bolton sat on a chair next to the bed at her side. Something was wrong.

"Hey, baby. I'm so glad to see you awake." Bolton placed his palm against her cheek.

"Hurt," was all she could manage to get out.

Bolton grabbed a bottle of something and handed it to Brandon. Then he helped her sit up while Brandon pushed two pills between her lips and held a glass of water to her mouth. She swallowed the pills with a little sputtering, but managed to get them down. She took a few more sips of the water and then turned her head away. Bolton eased her back down in the bed.

"I know your arm hurts, but how do you feel other than that?" he asked.

"Tired." Her voice came out in a husky whisper.

"Get some rest, Heather. When you wake up I'll get you some broth to eat. You need to eat something to fight the infection." Brandon stood up after squeezing her leg through the covers.

Heather wanted to know what was wrong with her arm, but couldn't keep her eyes open. The lids were so heavy. She closed them, but could hear everything going on around her.

"She's going to be okay, now," Bolton said.

"Yeah, she's going to be fine. I'm going to go cook up some chicken broth for her. She'll probably wake up again in a little bit. I want to get at least a few spoons of it in her. She's weak and needs the protein to heal."

"Thanks, Brandon. You know she would have died if you hadn't been here. I couldn't have taken care of her alone."

"You'd have managed."

Heather couldn't figure out what was going on. Why couldn't she remember what had happened to her? Something bad had to have happened for them to act like she'd almost died.

Several hours later, she managed to pry open her eyes again, and this time Brandon was in the room with her. He smiled when he realized she was awake.

"Hi there, sleepyhead."

"Hi."

"How are you feeling now?" He leaned forward in the chair.

"Better. My arm doesn't throb as bad as it did. What happened to me?"

"You don't remember?"

"No. I remember getting up and going into the bathroom to help you bathe. Then I can't remember anything after that."

"You were mauled by a wolf, Heather. We thought we had lost you."

"A wolf? Oh, God. How bad am I?"

"Your arm is pretty bad, but it's getting better."

She looked down toward where her arm lay on a pillow. She gasped at the sight of it. There were raised red lines with stitches all over her arm. She looked like a jigsaw puzzle. She attempted to move her fingers, and when they didn't move at first, she started crying.

"What is it, baby? Do you need something for pain?"

"I can't move my fingers."

"Shh, baby. They're probably just stiff. Hold on." He knelt next to the bed and carefully moved her fingers. Then he moved her wrist. "Okay, try and move just your fingers again."

Heather was afraid to try. She shook her head.

"You can do it. Move your fingers, Heather."

She drew in a shaky breath and willed her fingers to move. When they bent, she started laughing in relief. She looked up at Brandon and smiled.

"Told you. Now don't go moving your arm around. I want your stitches to heal straight as possible. We did the best we could, but they aren't perfect."

"I know you did. I'm sorry I worried you both so much." Her throat felt raspy and it was hard to talk. "Can I have something to drink?"

"Of course." He helped her to sit up then handed her a glass so she could hold it with her good arm.

She looked down at it and winced. "I even have some on this arm."

"Only a couple. Go ahead and drink up. You need to drink as much as you can. When Bolton gets back up here, I'll go warm up the broth and you can eat some."

"Where is Bolton?"

"He's finishing up chores. We've been taking turns sitting with you for the last four days."

"How did I get away from the wolf, Brandon?" she asked.

"Bolton got to you first, and grabbed it by the neck and tried pulling it off of you. It kept the wolf from getting to your throat. Then, when I got there, I had a gun. I shot him."

"Thanks for taking care of me, Brandon."

"You mean so much to me, Heather. I—"

Bolton burst into the room. "You're awake!" He hurried over to the bed.

"Hey, Bolton." She smiled up at him.

"I'm going to go fix that broth for you. I'll be right back." Brandon got up and left the chair for Bolton to sit on.

Heather went to reach for his hand, but cried out when she moved it.

"Hey," he said. "Don't move it."

"I wanted to hold your hand."

He reached across the bed and took her other hand and squeezed it. "I'll be right back."

She watched him disappear out the door then turned her attention to Bolton. He had a funny look on his face.

"What?"

"Nothing. What do you remember?"

"I really don't remember anything but getting out of bed the other morning. Then bits and pieces of hurting, until now."

"Well, all that matters right now is that you get well. We want you healthy again."

Heather felt like they were still keeping something from her, but try as she might, she couldn't remember, and it only gave her a headache to try. She had a feeling whatever it was would hurt her almost as much as the wolf had.

Chapter Eight

Several days passed, and it came time for her stitches to come out. Brandon dreaded doing it. It wouldn't feel good, but it shouldn't really hurt either, he hoped. Heather was a real trooper, and hadn't complained when they moved her and checked her arm and side each day. She still hadn't remembered anything, and he knew his time was running out. He needed to come clean with her before she remembered on her own.

"Okay, this is going to feel weird. It shouldn't really hurt though, so if it starts to hurt, tell me."

Bolton stood by with a garbage bag for him to drop them as he pulled them out. Halfway through, they all three needed a breather.

"It's not that it hurts, it just feels funny," she told them.

"That's okay. Just relax for a few minutes and we'll start again. So far it all looks good."

"Yeah, well, considering the alternative. I still look like a Frankenstein."

"I'm sorry, baby."

"Hey, I'm not blaming you at all. You saved my life. I just figure you won't like looking at it."

Bolton hurried to reassure her that they loved her no matter what. She stilled, and Brandon wondered if Bolton realized what he'd said. They'd never told her that before. Well, at least he hadn't. He didn't know what Bolton had told her.

"Okay, let's try this again." He bent over her arm and began clipping and tugging stitches loose.

"Bolton? Do you really mean it?"

"What, baby?"

"You said you loved me. Brandon?"

"We both love you, honey." Bolton brushed the hair from her eyes and bent over to kiss her.

Brandon swallowed his pride and smiled down at her. "I love you, too, Heather. You're my life."

"Why do I feel like something is wrong then? Did I do something stupid?"

"No!" they both said at the same time.

"You didn't do anything, baby. I did," Brandon confessed. "I'd really like to wait until you can sit up for a while before we talk about it, though."

Brandon held his breath. He could only hope she would wait and not make him talk about it just yet. He needed time, and she needed her strength back first.

"Okay, but as soon as I can sit up for more than fifteen minutes, I want to know what is going on."

"I promise, baby. I'll tell you everything. I just need you to be at your best."

"Now you're making me nervous." She looked from Brandon to Bolton and back again. "Am I going to be upset?"

"Yeah, baby. You're going to be upset, but not for long. I promise."

"I'm holding you to that."

Bolton insinuated himself between them and pushed Brandon back. "Everything will be fine, baby. You'll see."

Brandon grinned at the fact that Bolton wanted some alone time with her. He picked up the supplies and left them. He'd have his alone time later that night. Bolton was up for farm chores. He grinned and realized how much he was looking forward to spending time with her. To think that it could have been this way all those months if he'd only confronted her to begin with.

Then a thought struck him. What if she didn't accept his apology and explanation? What would he do if she rejected him? For all of a minute, his heart thundered in his chest at the thought, and his mouth grew dry. He honestly felt like he might pass out. Then the feeling passed.

No matter what happened, he would do everything in his power to make her happy. Even if it meant backing away. It would kill him inside, but he would do it for her happiness. Hopefully, her happiness would include him and Bolton both. Hopefully she would want them both equally, both in her bed and as a family, sharing the good times and the bad.

Brandon disposed of the trash and scalded the tweezers before putting them back in the first aid kit. Then he prepared supper for them. Heather was eating regular food now, and they were pushing her to eat every two to three hours, trying to build her strength up. He carried the tray up the stairs and walked in to find Bolton and Heather in a true lip-lock. He grunted, then cleared his throat. They came apart, panting.

"Don't you two think you should hold off on that for a few more days?"

"Nope," they both said, then chuckled.

"Well, I demand my kiss then." Brandon set the tray on the bedside table and leaned in for a kiss.

She didn't disappoint him, either. She opened to him immediately, and he plunged in like a man dying of thirst. It had been so long since he had truly kissed her. He ran his tongue around hers then slid back and forth in her mouth before nipping at her lower lip. She drew in a deep breath and sighed.

"Thanks," he said, equally winded.

"You're welcome." She winked at him.

"Now you need to eat."

Bolton stuffed several pillows behind her and waited in case she needed help. Brandon settled the tray in her lap and handed her a napkin. She smiled and dug in. He was happy to see her with such a good appetite. She'd lost a lot of weight over the last few months, and especially over the last few days.

He removed the dishes once she was finished, and took them back down to the kitchen. On his way back up he paused outside the bedroom when he heard Heather ask Bolton about why Brandon thought she would be mad.

"You need to let him talk to you about it, Heather. It's between the two of you. I'm not getting between you two."

She huffed out a breath. Brandon sighed. He needed to talk to her soon. Maybe he would carry her downstairs tomorrow and have the talk then. He made sure they knew he was coming in and smiled at her as soon as he walked in the door.

"How would you like to sit in front of the fireplace downstairs tomorrow for a little while?"

"Oh, can I?"

"Do you think she's ready for that?" Bolton looked dubious.

"She needs to sit up some to get her strength back. I won't let her sit up too long."

"Hey, you guys. I can talk for myself. I want to sit up some tomorrow."

Bolton and Brandon chuckled at her demanding tone. Brandon decided she was sounding more like her old self.

"If I'm going to be doing the morning chores tomorrow, brother, you get to do the evening chores tonight," he said with a mischievous grin.

"Fine. I'll do the chores tonight. Don't tire her out so that she won't feel like getting out of bed tomorrow." He gave Bolton an intense look, hoping it would tell him how important it was that he get her downstairs in the morning.

He left them and headed to the stables to tend to the horses. He wasn't sure how he was going to broach the subject yet. He just hoped some insight would come to him between now and in the morning.

* * * *

After eating breakfast, Heather was eager to go downstairs, and couldn't keep it out of her voice.

"Is it time yet?"

Brandon laughed nervously, but smiled and nodded. "Bolton is out doing chores. We'll make the most of the time we have."

He picked her up and carried her down to the lounge chair he'd prepared for her, complete with pillows and a blanket. He had the fire roaring, and a glass of water next to her. He also had a box of tissues next to the water as well. She seemed to notice all of it, and quirked an eyebrow at him.

"You really have me worried, Brandon."

"I'm not sure where to start, so I'm going to start at the beginning."

Brandon drew in a deep breath and walked over to the couch and sat down.

"When you first moved in with us, you were scared and uncomfortable around us. I knew I cared about you from the beginning, and I think Bolton was already in love with you before we ever made it back here. I was strict with you because I knew the dangers of living out here, not to mention the threat of someone grabbing you." He took a breath and continued.

"I treated you badly, and didn't realize it. You accused me of only wanting you to help around the house, and that I felt responsible for you, and that you belonged to me. You resented that, and we both said some insensitive things to each other.

"Over time, you obviously forgave me mine and tried to heal the rift between us, but I was resistant. I wanted you to love me despite that I felt like I needed to protect you. I wanted you to love me like you did Bolton, with no restrictions. I felt like a third wheel. I began to pull away from you. I foolishly thought you and Bolton would make a good team, and I was just in the way.

"I tried to move out, but knew I couldn't do it all at once. I slowly moved some of my things to the other room, and occasionally would stay up late and sleep in the other room without you realizing it. I don't even think Bolton knew it. We still had sex because I couldn't resist you, but I was trying to avoid that as well."

"You didn't care about me?" Heather's lips trembled.

"Yes, baby. I loved you. I loved you so much it hurt, but didn't think you really cared for me. I thought you were only going through the motions because you felt beholden to me. I wanted more than that."

"I didn't, though. I loved you as much as I loved Bolton."

"But we never said that to each other."

"No, we didn't. I guess that's why you were jacking off in the shower that morning."

Brandon closed his eyes. She had remembered after all.

"How long have you remembered?"

"Since last night, when I dreamed about it. It hurt so badly, Brandon."

"I know, baby. It was wrong on so many levels, but most of all because it hurt you."

"Why, Brandon? Why, when I was more than happy making love with you?"

"You have to agree, it wasn't making love. I fucked you. I tried to make it as impersonal as possible so that it wouldn't hurt so badly that you didn't really want me.

"When I jacked off, it was to thoughts of you loving me for me. It was of you loving me, and me loving you. I never thought about another woman, Heather. You have to believe me on that."

"Honestly, I don't know what to think. Do you really mean it when you say you love me?" Heather asked in a broken voice.

"Yes. I love you more than life itself. When I thought you were going to die, it nearly killed me. I didn't think I would be able to go on without you."

"Are you sure this isn't just guilt talking? That you feel guilty about it and what happened to me?"

"I'm sure, baby. I love you with all my heart. I want us to be a family. I want to move all the way back in, and make love to you as you're supposed to be made love to."

"I need to think about it, Brandon. It really hurt me finding you like I did. Knowing all those times that you didn't want to have sex was because you'd already taken care of yourself."

"Please, Heather. Please forgive me. I don't think I can function without your love."

"I do love you, Brandon, but I need some time."

"Do you want me to move out for now?" It nearly killed him to offer.

"No, I don't want you to move out. I just want some time to think about it."

He breathed a sigh of relief and went over to kneel beside her. He took both her hands in his and kissed them.

"Do you want to sit up for a little longer, or are you ready to go back to bed?"

"I want to sit up some more. I feel good sitting up. Just leave me to my thoughts for a little while, Brandon. I'll be fine in here."

"Okay, I'll check on you in an hour. If you need me before then, just call out. I'll be in the back washing clothes. They've sort of built up over the last few days," he said with a rueful grin.

"Let me be sick for a few days, and you let the house go to the dogs."

* * * *

Heather watched Brandon walk out of the living room and disappear around the kitchen wall. She could hardly believe what all he'd said. Still, it all made since in a twisted sort of way. She had said some nasty things to him, but he held a grudge and let it come between them. Could she forgive him of that? Could she erase the memory of him in the shower with his own hand around his cock? She just wasn't sure.

She could hear Brandon in the other room running water, and smiled. He seemed so earnest in his claims to love her. But she really wasn't convinced that it wasn't because he felt guilty about what happened. Maybe he blamed himself for her running outside and getting mauled by the wolf. What if she agreed to forgive him and months or maybe years down the road he realized he didn't love her?Could she handle that?

How did Bolton feel about all of it? She felt sure they had fought about it. Or did he even know what had happened? Now she doubted his love as well. What if they only cared about her because they were stuck with her? After all, they wouldn't have had her if she hadn't chosen their trailer to hide in.

Heather felt totally confused now. She began to doubt everything she thought she had known. Tears threatened to fall. She grabbed one of the tissues and blotted her eyes. She refused to cry now. It wouldn't help anything. It wouldn't help her make a decision that would affect them the rest of their lives. She felt the weight of everything sitting on her shoulders. She alone could decide their future, and it didn't seem fair.

Bolton walked in the back door and headed straight for her with a smile on his face. He seemed genuinely pleased to see her.

"Hey, Heather. How are you feeling?"

"I'm okay."

He frowned. "Are you getting tired? Do you want me to carry you back to bed?"

"No, I'm fine down here. It actually feels really good to be out of the bed."

"I guess you've been talking with Brandon, then."

"Yeah. We had our talk." She swallowed and looked down in her lap.

"Are you okay?"

"I'm not sure, Bolton. I feel all confused inside now." She sighed. "I just need some time to think."

"We'll give you all the time you need, baby. We just want you happy." Bolton's expression was careful.

Heather smiled a watery smile and held out her hand to him. When he took it, she squeezed it to let him know they were okay. Well, she hoped they were okay, anyway. She wasn't sure what to believe anymore.

Brandon walked through the living area toward the stairs carrying a set of sheets. He nodded at Bolton.

"Need some help with those?" Bolton asked.

"Yeah, thanks. I'm going to change the sheets while she's sitting up so they will be fresh when she lies back down."

Bolton squeezed Heather's hand one more time and smiled down at her.

"I'll be right back. We'll just be upstairs if you need anything."

"I'm fine. I'm enjoying sitting here in front of the fire. It's cozy." She forced a bright smile for his benefit.

She looked up at where Brandon stood with one foot on the stairs. He looked so forlorn standing there, like a little boy left inside while the others got to play. She felt sorry for him for a few seconds, then hardened her heart and reminded herself she had a lot to think about.

Something of her feelings must have shown on her face, because he sighed and turned to walk up the stairs. With that, she felt a little guilty. She needed to make a decision, but there was no need to torture him. He'd admitted his mistake and subsequent actions. He professed to love her. Surely that went a long way in her forgiving him.

Bolton followed Brandon up the stairs, leaving her alone with her thoughts again. She wasn't so sure that was a good thing. All she did was go around in circles in her head. Then she remembered something that was just as important. They were living together, no matter what happened. She had nowhere to go, and they didn't either. She couldn't separate two brothers, and couldn't live with one without the other one being in the same house. She needed to carefully think about her feelings. It affected all three of them, not just her and Brandon. Bolton would be affected no matter what her decision turned out to be. That knowledge sat heavily on her shoulders. She didn't want that power, because she held the power of devastation over all their lives.

Chapter Nine

Bolton grabbed Brandon's arm as they walked into the bedroom and turned his brother toward him.

"Did you talk to her? About everything?"

"Yes."

"And?" Bolton's stomach clinched in anticipation of the outcome.

"She's thinking about it. She doesn't know if she can forgive me or not."

"What are we going to do if she doesn't?" Bolton ran a hand over his head.

"We can't make her forgive me, Bolton. She feels whatever she feels."

"But where does that leave us?"

"I'll move into the next room. You will take care of her and love her like she deserves. I'll always protect her and do whatever I can to keep her happy. There isn't anything else we can do."

"It won't feel the same, Brandon. We're a team, all three of us. You screwed up, but people make mistakes. All families screw up, but they stay together and work through it." He helped Brandon pull the corners over the mattress. "I'll talk to her."

"No! Don't put any pressure on her. She doesn't deserve that."

Bolton watched the misery cross his brother's face before he covered it with a mask of determination. It broke his heart to know the two people he loved more than anything in the world were at odds. There had to be something he could do to mend the situation. Try as he might, though, he couldn't come up with anything.

They finished making up the bed in silence. Brandon plumped the pillows one at a time. When he got to the one he used, he hesitated, then laid it back in its place. No doubt he was contemplating if he would be sleeping there much longer. It felt like a knife in his gut to know things might not turn out how he wanted them to.

He was angry with his brother for screwing up in the first place, and wanted to bust his ass for it, but he was his brother and he loved him. They were all human and made mistakes, some worse than others. Brandon's had been a major breach of trust. No doubt Heather was feeling doubt now about how they felt about her. He included himself in that, because despite his having loved her all along, she would wonder if he only felt like he had to.

"She might not want either of us anymore," Bolton said in a near whisper.

"Don't think like that, Bolton. She's in love with you, and won't turn you away. You've been nothing but good to her, and treated her like a precious gift."

"But did I have to do that, or did I really love her like that?"

"Are you doubting how you feel about her now? Because if you are, you're a bigger fool than I was."

"No, I know I love her. But what is she thinking?"

"She's thinking that she loves you no matter what, and she isn't sure about how she feels about me anymore." Brandon gathered up the dirty sheets and headed out of the room toward the stairs.

Bolton followed behind him. When they made it down the stairs, it was to find Heather gone from the chair. They panicked. Brandon dropped the sheets and ran to the kitchen with Bolton right behind him. They found her sitting in a chair at the kitchen table.

"Why did leave the chair?" Brandon chided.

"We said we would help you if you called out." Bolton ran a hand over her head.

"I wanted to see if I could walk by myself. You've both carried me to and from the bathroom, and I don't like that. It's humiliating. I want to be able to go to the bathroom by myself."

Bolton felt her embarrassment, and could feel the heat rising in his face. He just hadn't thought about her needing to do it herself.

"You look winded though," Brandon pointed out.

Bolton shot him a dirty look. His brother needed to back off of being the naysayer all the time. It was one of the reasons Heather saw him in the light of her being a possession to him.

"It wasn't easy, but I made it and with practice, I'll do better. I'm getting my strength back." She smiled up at both of them.

Bolton felt his heart swell at her smile. She had included Brandon in it. Maybe things were going to work out, after all.

"Will you let me carry you back upstairs now? You really need a rest after all the activity," Brandon said.

She frowned, but nodded her head. "I am a little tired. I could probably take a nap."

"That sounds good," Bolton said. "Brandon, why don't you lie down with her while I finish up the clothes? Then you can do the chores tonight."

"I—I will if Heather wants me to."

Bolton heard the hesitation in his brother's voice. He looked at Heather to see what she would say.

She licked her lips and nodded.

"Are you sure?"

Bolton could have hit Brandon over the head. *Don't ask if she's sure, just do it. Idiot.*

She raised her arms out to him, and he smiled and gathered her into his arms, mindful of her wounds.

Bolton followed them up the stairs in case Brandon tripped. He would be there to catch them. Then he watched from the doorway as Brandon settled her into the bed beneath the covers. He sat on the edge of the bed and pulled off his boots and shirt, but left his thermals on. He lay stiffly beside her. Bolton shook his head and left them to work it out between each other. He couldn't do that for them no matter how much he wanted to.

Instead, he turned around and walked back downstairs to finish the laundry. With it being cold outside, he would need to hang it up in the living room in front of the fire. They kept a clothesline ready for that purpose. After hanging everything up, he eased upstairs to check on them. He couldn't help himself. He wanted to know that they were okay with each other.

When he peered around the door, he couldn't help but smile. Heather was lying across his brother with her head on his chest. Brandon had an arm around her waist. Maybe they hadn't started out that way, but their natural instincts had taken care of it for them. He hoped it would prove to be a balm for them to wake up that way. He wouldn't wake them up, even if it were time for Brandon to do the evening chores. He'd let them wake up on their own without his presence to complicate things.

* * * *

Heather felt movement beneath her face and the thump, thump sounds of a heartbeat. She was lying on top of Brandon. How had she gotten that way? She would have felt it if he had moved her, she was sure. She must have done it in her sleep. She'd naturally turned to him, knowing he would take care of her. Didn't that tell her all she needed to know?

"You awake?" he whispered next to her ear.

"You don't have to whisper. I'm awake." She went to move off him, but he tightened his arm around her waist.

"Could we just stay like this for a few more minutes? I love the feel of you in my arms."

"All right." Heather tried to remain relaxed and not stiffen up.

She must have done okay, since he sighed and cuddled her closer to him. She had to admit, it felt right. She snuggled against his chest and absorbed the warmth and scent of him. She hadn't really thought about it, but Bolton and Brandon smelled different. Not a lot, but enough that she would always be able to tell them apart.

Finally, he squeezed her a little tighter and eased her off of him. She immediately felt a loss. Not just of his body heat, but his presence.

"I better get up and see about the chores. It's getting late."

She turned over and watched him pull his shirt back on and step into his boots. He was a handsome man. She couldn't get over that he said he loved her. Surely he meant it. She wanted to believe he meant it.

"I'll send Bolton up so you won't be alone."

"That's okay. I'm fine. He's probably got things to do."

"I doubt he has anything more important than spending time with you." Brandon leaned over and kissed her.

His kiss was a gentle one, but she felt as if he were trying to tell her that he loved her through it. Maybe he really did.

Not long after he left her to go downstairs, Bolton appeared and stripped out of all of his clothes except the bottoms to his thermals. He climbed into bed with her and immediately snuggled close.

"Think you can sleep some more, or do you want to talk?" he asked.

"Hmm, right now, I just want you to hold me."

Bolton pulled her into his arms and kissed the corner of her mouth. Heather turned her face and kissed him back. She needed more, but she knew he wouldn't give it to her as long as she was *recovering* from her ordeal. Her arm did ache still when she used it, but not that badly. She wanted him to make love to her.

She felt him rub his hand up and down her back underneath her T-shirt. It felt so good to have that much skin-to-skin contact. She wanted more.

"Bolton, would you take off my T-shirt for me? I want to feel you against me."

"Are you sure? I'm afraid you'll get cold." He pulled back and looked at her.

"I'm sure. I won't get cold if you hold me close."

Bolton sat up in bed and carefully removed her T-shirt. When he lay back down, Heather crawled on top of him and laid her head on his chest. Her breasts pressed into him, and the warmth of skin-to-skin contact felt so good to her. She had missed it the last few days. His chest hair, sparse though it was, tickled her nose, and she smiled, giggling.

"What's so funny?"

"Your chest hair tickles."

"Do I need to shave it for you?" he asked, sounding completely serious.

"No, silly. I like it." She kissed his chest all over until he pulled her up to eye level and kissed her.

She reveled in the sheer beauty of his kiss. He was tender at first, but when she opened her mouth to him, he slid his tongue inside. Heslowly took her to another level of sensuality with the thrust of his tongue in and out of her mouth, mimicking what she wanted him to do to her pussy.

When he pulled back, they were both out of breath, with Bolton's face strained as if he were hurting. She figured out what it was all about when he pressed his hardened cock against her belly. That was what she wanted. She wanted to feel wanted, not feel like a burden.

"Bolton, make love to me. I want to feel your cock inside of me, filling me up. I don't want to feel empty anymore."

"Baby, I want to more than anything in the world, but not while you're still recovering. You need to heal first." The strain of holding back was evident in the tightening of his voice.

"I'm fine, Bolton. Please, don't make me wait any longer."

"You've only had your stitches out one day, Heather. Give it another few days, and I'll make you feel so good."

"I can't wait that long."

"Eat her pretty pussy, Bolton."

Heather jumped, then laughed. "I didn't hear you come in."

"Sorry, I figured you were too into each other to know it, but I couldn't wait to see if Bolton would give in to you. I don't think I could hold out against you."

Bolton smiled and slid down in the bed pulling the covers down as he went.

"Keep her warm, Brandon, while I taste her sweet cunt." He hooked his fingers around her panties and pulled them down and off.

Brandon smiled at her and began peeling out of his clothes. He left the bottoms of his thermals on, but climbed into the bed without a shirt.

"I don't trust myself if I take the bottoms off, and you don't need that sort of action yet."

Heather pouted. She had hoped to talk them into sex by rubbing up against their cocks. Still, the thermals had possibilities. They were soft, and if she played her cards right, they might still give in to her.

"I know that look, Heather. You've got something brewing in that devious head of yours. We are not fucking you tonight," Brandon told her, looking like a stern parent.

Heather scraped her nails down his chest, and he lost his stern look, trading it in for one of sensual arousal. She liked that look much better.

"No fair," he said in a strained voice.

It was at that moment that Bolton chose to lick her slit and brush his tongue against her clit. She shuddered and sighed in pleasure. She needed this. She needed them inside of her more, but this would do.

His tongue licked her like he was cleaning out the bowl of his favorite dish. Her juices began to flow the more he licked and sucked on her pussy lips. He spread them wide and shouldered her legs farther apart before he stabbed his tongue in deeper. Heather moaned and grabbed hold of Brandon's head to pull him down for a kiss. He let her and immediately pierced her mouth with his tongue.

Brandon used one hand to prop up, but put the other hand to perfect use as far as Heather was concerned. He began playing with her breasts, pulling on her nipples as she slowly began a long crawl up to heaven. When he pulled back from kissing her she whimpered, but he replaced his fingers with his mouth on her breast. With Bolton at her pussy licking her juices, and Brandon sucking on her nipple, Heather began to pant. God, she wanted one of them inside of her. Still, she wasn't going to complain now. They were making her feel so fucking good.

Bolton surprised her by adding two fingers to her cunt, already swollen from all of his attention to it. She groaned and lifted her hips to meet his slow thrusts.

"Be still, Heather. Let me do the work," he said.

"I can't be still."

"Brandon, can you hold her still?"

Brandon chuckled and placed the palm of his hands on her pelvis and held her still while his brother fucked her with two fingers, then turned his fingers up and explored her pussy to find that spot that drove her crazy. God, if he found that she would come for sure.

Less than ten seconds later, he found it and sent her flying off into nothingness. She was sure she screamed, but Brandon took her cry into his mouth, kissing her as she did.

They both soothed her as she came down from her flight into ecstasy. Brandon brushed her hair away from her face while Bolton rubbed her belly. She shivered, and they immediately changed positions and pulled the covers up over them. Right then, everything felt right in her world.

* * * *

"Do you think I could take a shower tomorrow? I want to wash my hair."

It came out of nowhere. Brandon was half asleep when she asked.

"Um, maybe. I guess. Your stitches are out, so I don't think there is any reason you can't.One of us has to be in there with you to be sure you don't give out and fall." Brandon squeezed her good shoulder.

"Maybe both of you could make sure I don't fall."

Brandon smothered a laugh. She was not giving up, and he realized in that moment that she had, in her own way, forgiven him. Did he need to hear the words? He wasn't sure, but he wouldn't push it right now. Now he would just enjoy the closeness they were all three feeling.

"What is she fussing about?" Bolton seemed to wake up at the end of the conversation.

"She wants to take a shower tomorrow."

"Umhmm, whatcha think?" Bolton's sleepy voice was muffled by the pillow.

"I said she could with us in the shower with her to be sure she doesn't fall."

"Okay. I'll wash her hair. You get to dry it."

"That's right, take the easy part," Brandon half grumbled.

"Well, neither one of you have to help me. I can do it all myself," she huffed.

"Oh, no, baby. We're going to make sure you get squeaky clean, and are safe in the process." Brandon laughed when she snorted at him.

"What's so hard about drying my hair anyway?"

"Nothing. I like drying your hair," Brandon confessed. He loved the sensual feel of it against his skin as it dried into spun silk.

"Let's go back to sleep," Bolton fussed.

Brandon and Heather looked at each other and laughed. She giggled, and he laughed because he didn't giggle. It felt good.

Everything felt good right then. He only hoped it would stay that way. He hoped this wasn't just a dream, or her way of getting back at him.She could be making him feel accepted then tell him she didn't love him anymore.

He frowned. She wasn't like that. Heather didn't have a vindictive bone in her body. She would never do that to him. If she was accepting him now, she would always accept him. He just had to make certain that he never gave her any reason to regret her decision to forgive him.

Chapter Ten

Three weeks later, they settled into their old routine of her working in the house and them working out on the farm. They checked in with her frequently, though. Bolton didn't like leaving her at all now, but they had to take care of the farm, or they would be without food and shelter. They didn't let her go out to the chickens or to milk the cow alone anymore before the sun was up. One of them always went with her. She didn't like it, but couldn't say much about it.

Bolton looked back toward the house from his vantage point on one of the fences he and Brandon were repairing. He longed to be there with her. But that wouldn't happen for hours yet. They needed to make it at least halfway around the fence line today to assure they didn't lose any more cattle.

There hadn't been any more snow to amount to anything, so they were fairly sure spring was on the way. Spring meant a lot more work for all of them. Between calving and planting the garden, they would be hard-pressed to get everything done. They would kill a couple of cows and smoke the meat to take it to Barter Town to trade for other things they needed. Maybe next year, they would have canned goods to trade as well. They'd eaten everything out of their small garden over the winter. They would be planting a larger garden this year, since they had Heather to work in it.

Bolton jumped down from the fence and picked up the tools to move on to the next section.

"Think she's okay?" he asked Brandon for the third time since they'd been out.

"She would fire the rifle if something was wrong. You know that."

"Can't help but be worried."

"I know, but we have to work. She's become a good shot with the rifle."

Bolton nodded, then cursed at the rotten wood of the next fence post. "This one will have to come out. Do we still have some timbers we can use to replace it?"

"Got two left. Have to cut some more tomorrow, I guess."

They dug the old post out and set in a new one. Then they worked on running the barbed wire to it. Bolton used the wire puller to keep the wire tight while his brother nailed the wire securely to the fence post.

"Okay, that takes care of that." Bolton ran a hand across his forehead to wipe away the sweat. Despite the cool weather, they had both worked up a sweat.

"Only another two hundred yards to go," Brandon teased.

"You can't tell me you aren't wanting to get back to her, too."

"Nope, I want to be snug inside that tight pussy of hers, but we have to be out here. Besides, she's busy taking care of the house."

"Everything is okay between you two now, right?" Bolton asked as he checked a post by kicking it.

"Yeah, everything is fine. I'm lucky as hell she's so forgiving. I don't know what I would have done had she chosen not to."

"What are we going to do when she gets pregnant?"

Brandon missed hitting a nail and tapped his thumb.

"Fuck!" He glared at his brother. "What did you say?"

"Unless both of us are sterile, it's going to happen. It's not like we miss a night between us."

"Hell, I really hadn't thought about it. I guess we have a kid."

Bolton chuckled at the look of worry on Brandon's face. He never would have thought Brandon would panic at the thought of children. Surely he wanted kids.

"Don't you want children?"

"Yeah, I love children. I just hadn't thought about having them. I mean we're just getting started as a family. Hopefully we'll have another year to settle in."

"We've already been here six years now. I think we're pretty settled by now, don't you think, brother?" Bolton asked with his tongue in his cheek.

"Smart-ass. I mean settle as a family. We've had a tough time starting off."

"I wonder what Heather thinks about kids, and if she's thought about getting pregnant?" Bolton looked off toward the house once again.

"Ah, hell. Go check on her, but don't stay too long. Get a quickie in if you have to, then come right back." Brandon took his hat off and wiped his forehead with the sleeve of his shirt before resetting it on his head.

Bolton smiled and took off running for the house. He slowed up once he was in viewing distance so if she saw him running she wouldn't think something was wrong. When he made it up to the back porch she was already outside waiting on him.

"What's going on?" she asked with a frown.

"Nothing. I wanted to see you."

She laughed and shook her head. "Naw, you wanted a quickie, is what you wanted. What if I said no?"

"Aw, baby. Don't say no. I ran all the way here just to get in that hot cunt of yours."

She sat her hands on her hips and mustered up a stern look. "Is that all I am to you? Somewhere to put your dick?"

"No, baby. I love your cooking, too," Bolton teased.

He growled and picked her up, carrying her in the house and up the stairs to the bedroom. She laughed all the way as he nipped at her chin and earlobes.

"Put me down, right now."

He complied by dumping her on the bed. She bounced then laughed and scrambled up to the top of the bed to hold on to the headboard.

"That's right. Hold on, cause I'm going to fuck you so good you're going to need something to hold on to." Bolton started unfastening his jeans after slipping out of his boots.

At the sight of him undressing, he watched her pink tongue slip out and lick her lips. He loved that she enjoyed sex as much as they did. He peeled out of his thermals and grabbed her legs to pull them down. She squealed and halfheartedly fought him. He managed to get her boots off and her pants unfastened and halfway to her knees.

"Bend over and let me fuck that hot little cunt of yours, baby."

"Bolton, you say the most romantic things to me." She giggled and rolled over to give him what he asked for.

"I'll whisper sweet nothings in your ear while Brandon fucks you tonight."

"Not if you're both doing it at the same time." She dropped a bombshell on him.

"What did you say?"

"You play with my ass all the time, but you've never taken me that way. I want to know what it feels like to have both of you inside me at the same time."

"Baby, are you sure?" Bolton's cock grew harder, if that were even possible.

He and Brandon had often talked about it, but never brought it up to her again, because they didn't want to push her into anything she didn't really want. Brandon would be in heaven if he knew he was having this conversation. He knew what it would feel like to be in her at the same time as his brother. She'd be so tight, it would literally squeeze the cum from their dicks.

"I'm sure, Bolton, or I wouldn't have brought it up. I've been daydreaming about it for weeks now. Can you convince Brandon for me? You know he won't do anything he thinks might hurt me. He's still holding back fucking me. I can tell."

"If you're really sure, I'll talk to him. Hell, I'll convince him, but you have to be sure, baby. You know it will sting and burn some at first."

"Nothing can hurt any worse than getting mauled by a wolf and then sewed up by a couple of farmers."

"There is that," Bolton said with a grin.

"So you'll talk to him for me?" she asked with a pout.

"I'll talk to him. Now turn around and give me that wet pussy. You're all but dripping over there. I'm about ready to shoot my load just thinking about it."

Heather giggled and turned back around. Bolton lined his straining dick up with her juicy slit, and pushed all the way in her with one long shove. She was so freaking wet. He slid right in. She moaned and began wiggling her ass.

"Move, Bolton. Do something."

He grabbed her hips and began pumping his cock in and out of her hot cunt. Her pussy squeezed around him as he started to pull out each time, as if resisting losing him. He tunneled in and out of her over and over until he was sure he wouldn't last much longer. When she reached between her legs, he figured she was going to finger her clit to make herself come, but instead, she tugged gently on his balls. That was all he needed. He shot her pussy full of cum with a loud roar. Never had he come so hard or so long. How in the world had she thought about that?

"Jeez, baby. That was awesome," he was finally able to say in a wheezy whistle.

She lay on her side, grinning.

"You didn't come though, and that's not acceptable." Bolton stretched out beside her and began fingering her clit. She gasped and grabbed hold of his head.

"Suck my nipples, Bolton."

He latched onto one of them and began sucking. He used his other hand to pinch and pull on the other nipple. It wasn't long before she was rising to meet his hand as he fingered her slit and rubbed over her clit. Then her eyes rolled back and she screamed her release. Bolton smiled, and wondered if Brandon had heard her. He wouldn't be worried because he knew Bolton was with her.

"I can't get enough of you, Heather."

"I can't get enough of either of you. I think about you whenever you're gone, and can't wait for you to get home. Do you think of me when you're out in the field or in the barn?"

"Hell, why do you think I'm here? Couldn't get you off my mind. Brandon and I fought over who got to come home and who had to stay and work the fences."

"And you lost," she teased.

"I think I won."

* * * *

By the time Brandon got back to the house, he was about to poke a hole through his jeans. Ever since Bolton had told him what Heather had said, he'd been so hard he could have pounded those nails in the fence without a hammer.

He found her bent over, checking something in the oven. He groaned at the sight of her delectable ass. Soon, he told himself. Instead, he waited for her to stand up again, and pulled her back into his arms where he kissed the side of her neck.

"Something smells delicious, and it isn't in that oven."

"Mmmm, you don't smell so delicious. I think you need a shower." She turned around and wrinkled her nose at him.

"You think he stinks now, wait until this summer," Bolton said as he walked inside.

"I bet you don't smell that good, either." She took a sniff and waved her hand in the air next to her nose. "You two need a shower before dinner."

Brandon laughed and gave her a spank on the ass as he passed her to head up stairs. He would use the spare shower while Bolton used the master bath. He planned to be nice and clean for his Heather. His Heather. It sounded so damn good to be able to say that without it meaning something different. She belonged to him and Bolton, but as their wife, not their possession, and now she knew it without a doubt.

After dinner, they sat on the couch with Heather between them, talking about what they'd accomplished during the day. The flames from the fire danced before them, flashing subtle lights in Heather's red hair.

"We'd have almost finished the fence line today if someone hadn't gone home halfway around," Brandon accused.

"If I hadn't, you would have."

"My point being, now we have to go back out tomorrow, and it will be my turn for a nooner." Brandon leaned around Heather to stick his tongue out at his brother.

"Okay, boys. If you don't play nice, neither of you will get anything." Heather laughed and stood up, pulling them to their feet.

"Let's go to bed. I'm thinking I might need a good, stiff…backrub tonight."

"I'll give you a stiff rub," Bolton teased.

Brandon forced her hand to his crotch and his throbbing cock. "I'm stiff enough for all of us, baby."

She rubbed her hand up and down the length of him through his jeans, then scratched her nails over the head of his dick through the material. He nearly came in his pants. Fuck, he was going to have to calm down, or he'd never last to even get in her tight ass.

They climbed the stairs one at a time, with her in the middle. Brandon watched her ass sway as she took each step after Bolton. He felt mesmerized by it, and nearly tripped when he came to the last step.

Bolton was already coming out of his boots and jeans by the time Brandon walked in the room. Heather laughed at the sight of his brother hopping around on one foot, trying to get his jeans off.

"You're going to break your fool neck like that, Bolton."

"Yeah, and you're not chomping at the bit."

Brandon rolled his lips inward to suppress a grin. His brother had no idea just how hard he was chomping. He sat on the bed and pulled off each boot before slowly standing up and unfastening his jeans. He prolonged the process just to prove to himself that he could. By the time he was down to his thermals, Bolton was all over Heather, sucking on her tits. Brandon groaned and nearly tore off his thermal underwear at the sight of Bolton's tongue licking those sweet nipples. He climbed up on the bed and crawled to plant his face between her soft thighs.

Heather moaned as he took his first lick of her delectable pussy lips. He delved between them with his tongue, then separated them with his fingers so he could lick up her tangy cream. He rolled his eyes upward to see Bolton pinching one nipple while he nibbled the other one. Then he took in as much of her breast as he could stuff into his mouth, and moaned around it. Heather hummed her approval.

He was going to make sure she came at least once before they took her. Then she was going to come as many times as he could make her. He wanted her to remember tonight as nothing but pleasure. He wasn't a fool. He knew that it would hurt at first, but he would make it feel good as soon as he was inside of her.

He inserted a finger into her cunt and searched for her G-spot. When he found it, he added another finger and softly brushed it over and over. Her keening noises grew in volume as she wound tighter and tighter on her way up to the top. Brandon pulled his fingers out covered in her sweet cream. He replaced them with the fingers from his other hand. Then he carefully inserted a finger inside of her little rosette, making sure to give her time to adjust before he added the second finger.

Bolton was feasting on her breasts, but snaked one hand down her belly to finger her clit as Brandon pumped his fingers in and out of both her pussy and her ass. He rubbed them together through the thin membrane separating them, and felt her begin to buck.

Heather started to tighten down on Brandon's fingers.

"She's ready, Bolton."

His brother pinched her nipple and her clit at the same time that Brandon added a third finger to her ass. She screamed and tightened down around both sets of fingers. They slowly stroked her down until she was panting, but breathing again. Brandon carefully removed his fingers and ran to the bathroom to clean up, and to grab a bottle of lube he'd gotten at their last trip to Skyline.

Bolton already had her straddling him, though not on his dick yet. He was kissing her and running his hands up and down her arms in a soothing rhythm. Brandon laid his hands on her shoulders and began massaging them to ease the tenseness from them. She was nervous, but also curious. She peered at him over her shoulder and smiled.

"I just need to catch my breath," she told him.

"You take all the time you need. I'm going to give you a back rub."

She leaned down over Bolton. He ran his hands up and down her back. Then he began to gently massage her shoulders and along her spine until she was limp and moaning.

Bolton looked up at him with a strained look on his face. Brandon lifted an eyebrow at the expression.

"You're rubbing her up and down my dick, man. It's already hard as hell."

Brandon full-out laughed and heard Heather chuckle, though halfheartedly. His brother narrowed his eyes at him.

"Come on, baby. Poor Bolton is in a hard way right now. He needs that slick cunt of yours around his cock." Brandon lifted her up to her knees.

Heather lifted her body from Bolton's abdomen and lined her pussy up with his stiff cock. She took him in one smooth drop. Brandon saw Bolton's eyes roll back in his head. He could well understand how it felt.

"Bend over some, baby. Put your head on Bolton's chest, and let me do all the work."

* * * *

Heather let Brandon push her down to Bolton's chest, and relaxed. She knew he wouldn't hurt her. Yeah, she knew it would burn at first, but he had promised it would feel good after that. She trusted him. She loved him. He'd told her often enough in the last few weeks that he loved her that she believed him now.

When he squirted something cold on her back hole, she shivered. He laughed, and then rubbed the jelly-like substance around her hole before slowly pushing in a finger. It didn't hurt, as they had been playing like this for awhile. She didn't even mind the second finger when he pushed it in next. He moved them around and pumped in and out of her ass with them until he seemed satisfied. Then he pulled out and squirted the cold stuff into her ass and pushed three fingers inside of her. She yelped but didn't pull away. It burned.

"Easy, baby. Push out and relax, like before."

He didn't move at first, then slowly began to push them farther in and pull them out. She did what he said, and pushed out as he pushed in. He began a slow rhythm of push and pull until she began thrusting with him.

"Okay, baby. I think you're ready."

"Thank God. Do you know how hard it is to be still with my dick in her tight pussy?"

"Shut up, Bolton," his brother said.

Heather felt him pull his fingers free, then a few seconds later, the head of his cock began pushing against her back hole. She remembered what he had said and began to push out to let him in. It stung. She whimpered, but she continued to press out until, with a pop, he was inside past the tight ring. He remained still for a few seconds to let her pant through the initial pain. Then he began a slow pump, with Bolton pulling out at the same time he was pushing in. They struck up a rhythm of push and pull until she was wild with need.

"Oh, God. Faster, harder. Something!" She tried helping them, but couldn't manage the rhythm.

"Easy. Let us do all the work. Just feel, baby."

Brandon adjusted his stance, and his thick cock brushed over nerve endings she hadn't known she had. She felt stuffed full of cock. With both of them pumping inside of her, she didn't have a chance not to climax. Every spot in her body was being stimulated. Even her clit was rubbing against Bolton's pubic hair. She could feel them rubbing against each other through that thin membrane. It was so erotic she felt like crying. She had never cried during sex before, but tears began to fall as she hurdled up a long line of electrical energy that grew out of her body to stop and prance along her clit and her nipples. She wasn't going to be able to survive. She began to panic.

"I can't stand it."

"Are we hurting you?" Bolton stopped.

"No, no! Don't stop! Please, don't stop. It doesn't hurt. It's going to kill me. It feels too good. I can't handle it. Oh, God." She thought she would explode when her climax hit her. She stiffened up and felt the men follow her as she tumbled over and over into bliss. Their loud shouts sounded a million miles away. She had no idea if she made a sound or not because she couldn't think, only feel.

After what seemed like hours, she began to breathe and hear again. Brandon and Bolton were both lying next to her, rubbing up and down her arms, talking to each other.

"There she is," Brandon said when she opened her eyes again.

"You passed out on us. I was worried," Bolton said.

"Dear God. I've never." She tried to think what to say and couldn't.

"It's okay. We've got you, baby." Bolton kissed her lightly on the lips. "Just rest."

She turned to look up at Brandon and smiled. "I've never felt so possessed in my life."

"I hope it's a good sort of possession," he said.

"The best."

Chapter Eleven

Spring found them all working hard from sunup to sundown. Heather spent most of her days in the garden, but she carried a gun with her everywhere she went. She had turned out to be a very good shot.

They had enlarged the garden to include enough for her to put up vegetables for the winter and possibly to trade at Barter Town. She hated going there, but they couldn't leave her alone on the farm, and it wasn't safe for only one of them to go, so she wrapped a sheet around her head so no one would really see her. She felt like a Bedouin woman.

Spring passed, and summer parched them with a vengeance. They were lucky to have a small stream running through their farm. It didn't dry up, but it got very low. She pumped water from one of the wells to water the garden and managed to keep it alive. The men helped her when they weren't busy in the field with the animals or the hay.

Early one morning, she woke up feeling sick. She made it to the bathroom just in time to throw up. It felt like her insides were going to come up. It wasn't long before she had both men in the tiny space with her. She couldn't breathe.

"I need some room. Please," she panted.

They backed up, but didn't leave her. Brandon grabbed a bath cloth and dampened it before handing it to her.

"Wipe your face and cool off. You'll feel better."

Bolton looked as if he didn't know what to do. Heather felt sorry for him. None of them had been sick since she'd been attacked by the wolf. He didn't know how to handle it. She tried a smile, but even that much movement churned her gut. She wiped at her mouth and face and then leaned back against the wall for support.

"What can we do for you?" Brandon asked. He had a strange look on his face.

"Nothing. I just need to rest a minute. I must have a virus or something." She already felt a little better, but really wanted to lie down again.

"How about if we carry you to bed? Do you think you would feel better lying down?" Bolton asked.

"Yeah, that would be nice. Help me up. I can stand now, I think."

"Don't move," Brandon said. "Let Bolton carry you back to bed. I'm going to go get you some crackers."

She frowned at him. Why would she want crackers when she'd just thrown up? She let Bolton pick her up and carry her back to bed. He climbed back in bed with her and cuddled around her. It felt good to feel his warmth at her back. She no longer felt nauseous, but didn't feel up to getting up yet, either.

Brandon walked back in the room carrying a glass of water and a sleeve of crackers.

"Here, try a cracker. It will settle your stomach." He handed her a cracker and held the glass of water for her.

"Brandon, I don't think I can manage to eat anything."

"Just trust me and try one." He waited while she took a small bite, then handed her the water to wash it down.

He nodded for her to take another bite. Before long she had finished the cracker and half of the water. She felt fine, but sleepy. Maybe there was something to the cracker after all. He folded the paper around the crackers and left it on the bedside table on his side. Then he climbed back in bed. Heather snuggled up to his warm belly and dozed lightly. She knew when they got up to go to work, but decided to stick to the bed for a little while longer. She felt okay, but was tired.

Finally, she realized she needed to get up and get dressed. She felt fine now. No more upset stomach. She wasn't sure what had been wrong, unless it had just been a fluke. She hated that she hadn't gotten the men their breakfast, but she would have lunch ready for them.

She had just put the sandwiches on the table when Brandon and Bolton walked through the back door laughing.

"What's so funny?"

Brandon looked over at Bolton and started laughing again. Heather put her hands on her hip and gave them both a stern frown.

"Nothing really. We're just laughing about some of the things we used to get into as kids."

Heather smiled and shook her head. They didn't talk about their pasts much. She didn't, either. It hurt to remember her family and friends were all gone. She preferred to think about her future with her men.

After lunch, they both hugged her and left her to work in the garden while they returned to the field.

"Don't get too hot out here." Brandon warned her. "Maybe you got too hot yesterday, and that's why you were sick this morning."

"Maybe so. I didn't feel sick when I went to bed, though." She shrugged and grabbed her things to go outside. She stuck her gun in the waistband of her jeans and closed the kitchen door behind her.

That night they talked about plans for the farm over the next year, and how they could improve things around the house. She got so hooked up in hearing their plans, she didn't even think about having been sick that morning. They headed to bed and she fell right to sleep.

The next morning, Brandon woke her up and made her eat a cracker. She felt a little icky and wasn't sure about eating, but figured it had made her feel better the day before.Maybe she wouldn't get sick this time at all. She drank the water and fell right back to sleep.

* * * *

"Told you," Brandon said as he and Bolton ate their breakfast later that morning.

"She's going to flip when she figures it out," Bolton said.

"I don't think we need to let her go too long without suggesting it to her. She needs to take things slower and get plenty of rest. You know how she pushes herself to work in the garden." Brandon didn't want her to run herself down.

"How do we tell her though?"

"Tell me what?" Heather stood in the doorway with her hands on her hips and a worried expression on her face.

Brandon jumped up and pulled her into his arms. "How are you feeling this morning?"

She frowned at him and pulled away to glare at them. "Tell. Me. What?"

"Don't look at me. You're the boss. You tell her." Bolton threw his hands up in the air.

Brandon frowned at him then turned back to face Heather with her now angry expression. How was he supposed to say it? Maybe the direct approach was the best one.

"Heather, baby. We think you're pregnant."

Bolton was the one who caught her before she hit the floor in a dead faint.

"Well, I guess that was one way to tell her," Bolton fussed.

"Let's get her on the couch." Brandon led the way to the living room.

By the time Bolton had her tucked on the couch, she'd come to and was staring at them as if they'd gone crazy.

"Did you say you think I'm pregnant?"

"You've been sick the last two days. If I'm thinking right, you haven't had a period in a couple of months, either." Brandon waited for her to think it through.

"I guess I didn't know you kept up with my periods." She turned red at the mention of it, then shook her head.

"What, baby?" Bolton asked.

"What am I going to do if I am? I don't know how to take care of a baby."

"I guess we'll learn together." Brandon sat on the couch and pulled her back into his arms. "We'll do fine. You'll have both of us to help with everything."

"Oh, God!" Bolton exclaimed.

"What?" Brandon asked, wishing his brother hadn't scared Heather.

"Who's going to deliver the baby?"

"I guess that will be Brandon, since you look like you're going to faint," Heather said.

"Well, everyone, looks like we need to plan another trip to Skyline. We need baby supplies and to raid a bookstore on babies and birthing." Brandon figured being prepared was their best bet. Besides, he needed to keep Bolton busy, or his brother was going to have a heart attack thinking about it.

"There's a mall there," Bolton pointed out after drawing in a few deep breaths. "I bet there's everything we need there for babies and maternity clothes and books."

"We'll need to get diapers from Walmart though." Heather seemed to be getting past her initial shock.

"Okay, let's make a list of things we need to get and where to get them. Then we'll plan a trip for the end of the week. That should give us time to finish what we're working on. It's still light at eight, so we'll have plenty of time if we get an early start." Brandon eased Heather off his lap and stood up.

"I'll make a list and then you two can look over it and add whatever I'm missing." Heather sat up.

Bolton quickly moved to help her stand. She laughed.

"I may be pregnant, but I'm not helpless. I can still do things. I'll just eventually get slower at it," she said.

"Brandon, she doesn't need to work in the garden anymore. We're going to have to divide our time between it and the fields."

"Brandon, stop him before he says something he's going to regret." Heather frowned at Bolton.

"Bolton, let's go on out to work. She's fine right now. We need to talk, brother."

* * * *

It took a few weeks, but Heather finally convinced Bolton she wasn't going to break either working in the garden or in the bed. They pored over the baby books they'd gotten in Skyline along with all the baby stuff they could haul. They were setting up a nursery in the bedroom next to theirs, but the baby would sleep in their room to begin with.

"I swear, it didn't look that hard to put together in the instructions," Bolton fumed.

He and Brandon were putting together the baby bed and other furniture they had gotten from the baby store in the mall.

"I told you to get the ones already put together."

"There wouldn't have been as much room, and we needed the room, baby." Bolton looked at the directions again and shook his head.

"I'm going downstairs so I don't have to listen to all the cussing you two are doing. It's not good for the baby to hear it at this stage in development."

Brandon snickered. Bolton looked as if he believed her. She shook her head and carried the books she was reading downstairs to the living room. They were enjoying the rainy afternoon together for a change. She enjoyed having them around her even with their cussing the baby bed with every curse word they could make up.

Bolton had a lot of adjusting to do. He still worried every time she groaned or walked outside. He fussed at her for climbing on the ladder in the pantry and for working in the garden. Brandon stood back and let her do whatever she wanted within reason. He put his foot down at riding horses while she was pregnant. It was fine. She didn't really want to ride them anyway. She'd just wanted to see where he would balk.

They treated her like the most important thing in their lives. She made little changes to the house here and there. It felt so good—like a real home. She wanted everything to be perfect for when the baby came because she knew once they had a baby to deal with, everything would change for all of them.

Brandon walked down the stairs to where she was standing looking out the window. He pulled her back into his arms and placed a hand over her little belly.

"How are you doing?"

"I'm fine. Just thinking about how far we've come since I hitched a ride with you."

"Do you regret you hitched your wagon to ours?"

"Not even a little bit."

Brandon rubbed her belly. "I'll be glad when you get a little baby bump I can rub and talk to."

"Yeah, you say that now, but wait until it's big enough I can't see my feet, and I'm moody and cry all the time."

"Is that what that book is telling you?" he asked.

"Yep. Being pregnant is going to be just as hard on you two as it is on me."

"I already figured that out."

She elbowed him in the stomach, and he chuckled. Bolton stomped down the stairs, muttering to himself.

"Here you are. I thought you were coming back up to help me."

"Got sidetracked," Bolton said, nuzzling the side of Heather's neck.

He walked over to where they were standing looking out the window. "What are we looking at?"

"Our lives in a few years," Heather told him.

"How do you mean?"

She grabbed hold of him and pulled him over next to her. The three of them looked out the window at the flowers in the front bed and the drive heading out toward the road.

"Just remember this moment, and every year for the rest of our lives, we'll look out this window and remember when we were young." Heather squeezed both of their hands and smiled. She loved her men—both of them.

THE END

WWW.MARLAMONROE.COM

ABOUT THE AUTHOR

Marla Monroe lives in the southern part of the United States. She writes sexy romance from the heart and often puts a twist of suspense in her books. She is a nurse and works in a busy hospital, but finds plenty of time to follow her two passions, reading and writing. You can find her in a bookstore or a library at any given time when she's not at work or writing. Marla would love for you to visit her at her blog at themarlamonroe.blogspot.com and leave a comment or write her at themarlamonroe@yahoo.com.

Also by Marla Monroe

Ménage Everlasting: Men of the Border Lands 2:
A Home with Them
Ménage Everlasting: Men of the Border Lands 3:
Their Border Lands Temptress

For all other titles, please visit
www.bookstrand.com/marla-monroe

Siren Publishing, Inc.
www.SirenPublishing.com

Lightning Source UK Ltd.
Milton Keynes UK
UKHW020503051118
331786UK00011B/169/P